HIGH F

for *Songs of My Selfie: An A   ~~~~ ~~~~~*

"Rather than trying to shake off the stereotypes thrust
upon them by a dying generation, the authors of
Songs of My Selfie wear their flaws on their shoulders and
dare you to mention them. If you want a preview
of some writers with brighter futures than the
newspapers anticipate, well, here you go."

JF Sargent, Editor, Cracked.com

"Well, this book is like a kick in the nuts. Bad news first:
nothing makes you feel older than reading very good stories
written by very young writers. At the same time, nothing is more
exhilarating. The stories collected here are sharp, funny, and,
dare I say it, wise. This is the book you want to read if you are
curious about who'll be driving the truck in a few years."

Ethan Rutherford, Author, *The Peripatetic Coffin and Other Stories*

"For a generation of screen addicts, these millennials
sure can write. Constance Renfrow and crew
give me faith in the future."

Mickey Hess, Author, *The Nostalgia Echo*

"Wry tales that yearn, squirm, and slam."

Ron Dakron, Author, *Hello Devilfish!*

"Alternates between snapshots of self-doubt,
self-discovery, and self-determination.
It's sweet and confident and deft and challenging."

Zac Hill, Chief Innovation Officer, The Future Project;
Former Lead Game Designer, Magic: The Gathering

"Prophets of the end times, just looking for a way forward."

Ben Loory, Author,
Stories for Nighttime and Some for the Day

Songs OF MY SELFIE

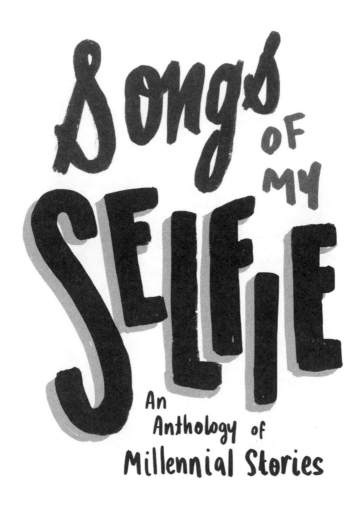

Songs OF MY SELFIE

An Anthology of Millennial Stories

Edited by Constance Renfrow

Foreword by Meagan Brothers, author, *Weird Girl and What's His Name*

THREE ROOMS PRESS
NEW YORK, NY

Songs of My Selfie
AN ANTHOLOGY OF MILLENNIAL STORIES

EDITED BY
Constance Renfrow

ISBN 978-1-941110-40-9 (print)
Library of Congress Control Number: 2015955344

"The Edge of Happiness" by Constance Renfrow was first published in the *Franklin & Marshall Alumni Arts Review*, April 2015.

COVER DESIGN:
Victoria Bellavia
www.victoriabellavia.com

INTERIOR DESIGN:
KG Design International
www.katgeorges.com

DISTRIBUTED BY:
PGW/Perseus
www.pgw.com

Three Rooms Press
New York, NY
www.threeroomspress.com
info@threeroomspress.com

for millennials
and
anyone who knows what it is to have
a quarter-life crisis

CONTENTS

FOREWORD

BY MEAGAN BROTHERS

Back in the day, a lot of Baby Boomers liked to remind us young Gen-X slackers that their superior generation had initiated a cultural and sexual revolution, and made better music to boot. But the utopia that should have come along after the magical sixties was in fact a fraught landscape of political and social quagmires: Watergate, Vietnam, homeless vets, skyrocketing divorce rates, Iran–Contra, Jimmy Swaggart, yuppies, cocaine, and a lot of glossy hair metal. No wonder one of the most popular television shows of the early nineties was a paranoid conspiracy drama that advised viewers to *trust no one.* No wonder Kurt Cobain appeared on the cover of *Rolling Stone* with the words CORPORATE MAGAZINES STILL SUCK Sharpied on his T-shirt. Sarcasm and irony ruled the day. Our generation saw the crumbling façade of what the Baby Boomers had wrought and we were, as they say, over it.

But our cultural burnout was nothing compared to what millennials are facing. A post-9/11 world of even deeper mistrust, a seemingly endless war, economic collapse, racism, xenophobia, escalating gun violence, cyberbullying, crystal meth, crushing student debt, and ever-more-rapidly melting ice caps. It's enough to make you want to throw up your hands and quit. Or maybe just throw up.

The young authors in this collection, however, have only just begun. Their work fearlessly tackles this world head on. Some crusty old Gen-Xers like to complain about the kids today. *All they do is text and take selfies while the world burns.* But consider the selfie. To turn the camera on ourselves is to look at ourselves unflinchingly, but also under our own direction. We take control of our own image when we take a selfie. And maybe there's a certain power in that; an assertion of self-reliance that would do Emerson proud.

Consider these stories as selfies. Seventeen tales, seventeen defiant, purposeful snapshots of life in a precarious world. Each of these authors is showing you something new, with a viewpoint that is uniquely their own. They are meeting the challenges of this world head on, without fear, without looking away. Now, they reveal these snapshots to you. Take a look. ◻

▶ **CONSIDER
THESE STORIES
AS SELFIES . . .
SEVENTEEN TALES,
DEFIANT, PURPOSEFUL
SNAPSHOTS OF LIFE
IN A PRECARIOUS
WORLD.**

I CELEBRATE MY SELFIE . . .

INTRODUCTION BY CONSTANCE RENFROW

illennials. Twenty-somethings. Unique little snowflakes. We take selfies and Instagram our food, and on a particularly eventful day we might live-Tweet someone else's breakup. I can't exactly blame anyone for thinking it: we certainly sound obnoxious, don't we?

Fortunately, there are plenty of resources out there on how to deal with us—and how to deal with being us. Sites like Buzzfeed and Huffington Post provide weekly encouragement—usually in listicle form ("25 Crippling Self-Doubts We All Have When We're 25!"). Magazines and books explain to our parents everything they did wrong that's now preventing us from moving out and getting our own insurance. Even our bosses seem to need help engaging us, their millennial employees—who apparently won't do anything unless we're told exactly how it benefits us. Or at least, this is the sort of thing that's exploding on our news feeds (and so it must be true, right?).

But to hell with that. At Three Rooms Press, co-directors Kat Georges, Peter Carlaftes, and I (their millennial-aged editor) are inspired by the passion of young creative types, and their ambition and drive. We believe today's literary community needs to celebrate the spark that millennial writers have—much the same spark all young writers have had for centuries. We want to provide a platform from which up-and-coming writers can share their work with their peers, as well as with past and future generations.

We created *Songs of My Selfie* to be an anthology of stories by millennials, about millennials, for millennials. It features seventeen new writers under the age of twenty-six (that bittersweet year when the final advantages of early adulthood have been used up), with a cover designed by a twenty-something typographer. All of the stories chosen for inclusion came from our "Quarter-Life Crisis" contest, held over the summer of 2015. The goal was to create an anthology that showcases the talent, creativity, and dreams of young writers and characters of all genders, ideologies, creeds, sexualities, religions, backgrounds, etc., while speaking to a common experience new to our generation: the quarter-life crisis.

"Quarter-Life Crisis" is the theme of this anthology, and it is defined by that pillar of accuracy and wisdom, Wikipedia, as: *a period of life usually ranging from the late teens to the early thirties, in which a person begins to feel doubtful about their own lives, brought on by the stress of becoming an adult.*

Or in plainer language, it's that moment when a recent grad realizes that sleeping on a leaky air mattress next to her Craigslist roommate is just the *worst*. Or when a newly minted Master of American Literature gets the first paycheck of his dream career and discovers it won't even cover that month's rent. Or when a twenty-three-year-old mother comes to terms with the fact that she hates her husband—and the new home they just bought together.

In short, this is the time when we fear we'll never become fully functional adults—or worse, that maybe adulthood just never gets better at all. The quarter-life crisis affects everyone differently, and sometimes the only thing you can do about it is write. Our hope is to show our fellow millennials that no one's alone—that we're all experiencing this together—and to clear up our dreams, fears, and real-life experiences for anyone who wants to understand what being twenty-something in 2016 is actually like. ⬛

Songs OF MY SELFIE

suzanne herman

SUZANNE HERMAN is a recent graduate of Barnard College in New York City, where she majored in English. She is currently pursuing all forms of literary involvement. Suzanne's work has appeared in *Rainy Day Magazine* (Fall 2015) and the anthologies *Connected: What Remains as We All Change* (Wising Up Press, 2013) and *Dumped* (She Writes Press, 2015). She is the winner of the Howard M. Teichmann Writing Prize, the second-place winner of the Peter S. Prescott Prize for Prose Writing, and a finalist for the Southampton Review Comic Fiction Prize, judged by Daniel Menaker (2015).

THE MOST LAID-BACK GUY EVER

t seemed like the unlikeliest place to see The Most Laid-Back Guy Ever. If you can be laid-back in an airport lounge, you've really got the act down. I'd been airborne for the last thirteen hours, Tokyo to JFK, and I'd eaten only freeze-dried ramen noodles and salted peanuts. I was holding an oversized water bottle marketed to panicky, dehydrated travelers who don't know what money in their pocket is real anymore. My mind was spinning in recirculated air and my left leg had only just recovered from pins and needles. My boss and I had separated at gate J3—he on his way to a hotel for a shower and a nap, me onto the much cheaper midday flight back to Chicago. When you've been staring at someone for a majority of the previous five days, it feels oddly sentimental to say goodbye.

"Thank you for your help this week," he'd said. But he'd been looking at his phone.

"Of course," I'd said. Which isn't really a response.

My world had undoubtedly shrunk; I could not now imagine an existence where I would not be seeing this high, perspiring forehead for two whole weekend days. But so it was, and it contributed highly to the giddy, almost drunk feeling that propelled me to the next gate. When I got there, I became a puddle in the black leather seat. I did not sit up straight and I did not cross my legs. I pushed my hair *into* my face.

When I was done rebelling, I adjusted my watch, ran my tongue over the grime of my teeth, and took out a book, all before I looked up and saw him sitting across the carpeted aisle. When you're under thirty but above twenty, female, straight, and have hurried in order to sit and wait in an airport, there are sights that will stop you like a bird into a window. A kitten will stop you, like it always will, but so will a cute boy of more or less your age.

He was dressed like you want a guy to be dressed, so picture that. His shirt was blue cotton and button-up, but it billowed slightly around him, like it was gauze and he the beach. His brown pants hit just short of where they were probably supposed to. He was wearing desert boots without socks and without the laces. Next to him was a traveler's backpack, the kind you use for hiking and for looking like an interesting person. The side pocket was stretched into the shape of hardcover books, a small stack. The backpack's green-and-gray surface was scratched and dirtied in all the right places. The kind of dirt collected by running for trains or sitting on camels. I looked down at my roll-aboard, black and spotless. What is it about people whose objects have so clearly lived? Why does it make it seem as if they have lived more recklessly, with more consequences good and bad, than those of us who keep our backpacks clean?

He was sunk fashionably low in his black leather seat, his knees almost parallel to his chest and both feet flat on the floor. He had a wide, welcoming face. His eyes were open and yet filled with a pleasant sleepiness, lightly fixed to a spot on the wall to his right, my left. He had a set of teeth like you've never seen.

Take me to that place, Most Laid-Back Guy Ever, where sitting in the waiting area of an airport is the easiest, most enjoyable thing you've ever done. To that place where life rushes over you like a lukewarm flood, like a bath.

A GIRL WALKED UP AND PUT her things next to his. She wasn't laid-back enough to be his girlfriend. Her face was slightly sweaty and possessed none of the effortlessness of the man I couldn't take my eyes off of. Besides, she just wasn't pretty enough to be sleeping with this guy.

From my seat less than five feet away I was performing. I tried to sink coolly into my seat, but it came out more like a slouch. My shoes didn't have laces but if they did I definitely would have taken them out, just to see how it worked. Maybe if I concentrated hard enough on ridding myself of all worldly cares, I could get his phone number. But the same four walls of one-way glass that had been dropped around me at birth—or at the very least when I started working for Mr. Hickman—continued to do their work. I could see them, those two, over there, and if I paid attention I could hear what they were saying, but their eyes never drifted toward me. You would think, statistically speaking, that in the course of their conversation one of their collective four eyes would notice me, glance in my direction even accidentally. I was staring rather intently now. Maybe if I coughed, or let out some sort of howling noise.

I chose, this time, not to be offended or surprised. Instead, I took it as a gift. I took it as a gift because I could feel, like you can feel a plane lifting in the bottom of your stomach, that this man was one I should watch undisturbed. He was the group of girls at the neighboring lunch table in high school, or the man in the sharp suit talking on his cell phone where he thinks you can't hear: this guy knew something I wanted to know.

"WHATEVER HAPPENED TO THAT GIRL I met?" The Friend of The Most Laid-Back Guy Ever was asking.

"Which girl?"

"The Russian model or actress or something."

He snorted. Not harshly or meanly, just an easy exhalation through his nose that wasn't quite a sigh. Textbook snort. "Talia? She was a fashion blogger."

"Fashion blogger. Right." The friend gave a snort that actually was kind of mean. "What happened to her?"

"We stopped hanging out. She was great, really beautiful and smart . . ."

I thought: *yep.*

". . . but things fell off. I mean, I still talk to her some-times, I guess." And then he gave an easy laugh. Joy rolling over his face like wind. As he laughed, he pushed his hair back. It was the first time I'd seen him adjust himself, as if he hadn't been aware of his own existence until now. I stopped twisting my hair.

"You know how it goes," he added about the fashion blogger.

I really, truly didn't. Teach me how to wear my shoes without laces and lie around like the world is one big picture window for looking through. Teach me, oh prophet of ease, how to talk about breakups like they're sick days: too bad really, but there's always tomorrow. This kind of insight, I thought, is why you should always hurry to catch planes, even if you'll always be early.

"When's the interview?" The friend asked.

"Not positive. I have it in an e-mail."

"You nervous?"

"Nah. I'll get it or I won't."

"Right. But it would be nice to be in Chicago for a while. Closer to Mom and all that."

He nodded impossibly slowly. Watching him nod was like watching a candle on the boarder of lit and unlit. Was his head actually moving downward, pausing, and moving back, or was it an illusion caused by the light?

"I think you'll get it," Must-Be-His-Sister said, and I agreed. I may even have nodded at them from across the way, a quick and bobbing nod that was much too eager. I would hire him. If only to have him sit at the desk next to me, in the already crowded space outside Mr. Hickman's office, and serve as a reminder that, really, in the grand scheme of things, there is nothing to worry about. Not my career or my likability or my performance evaluation next Friday or my dog's expensive food. We are all just passengers waiting for a flight to Chicago in order to sit for a job interview that may or may not mean we'll spend more time with our mothers, when you think about it.

▯

THE TRIP TO JAPAN HAD been pointless. As a personal assistant I accepted all of my boss's anxiety with none of the reward. The first night, I set three alarm clocks and then didn't sleep. During the days, I sat in the lobby of corporate office buildings and waited to be needed. I held my cell phone in my hand, and yet somehow I was still unprepared for the intermittent beeping and buzzing, jumping in my seat each time. I got coffee. I wrote a lot of things down. I nodded my head. I stared at the glass and black metal of that city, the tide of men in navy blue weaving through it. I heard Japanese like a ringing in my ears. The whole thing gave me stress dreams about robots and indigestion from eating too much rice.

The return trip had just been depression spread across two continents. A ball made of steel wool had appeared in my chest. On the plane ride back I'd developed the charming habit of ironing the spot above my breastbone with the palm of my right hand. I'd press down until the pounding stopped, then sweep left to dislodge the feeling. It hadn't worked, and I could feel the ball gathering new materials to fortify itself as we crossed the ocean. It was made now of wire and bits of bone. Also the tinsel you put on Christmas trees. All of it had been twisting and rotating behind my sternum, until I sat down in the waiting area.

I wasn't attracted to The Most Laid-Back Guy Ever; at least it wasn't entirely that. But I definitely would have made out with him, had he asked.

▯

Sister to The Most Laid-Back Guy Ever got up again, probably to use the restroom. I had to go too, since I had by now finished the giant bottle of water. I'd been taking quick, almost panicked sips as I listened, afraid to miss anything. But if he wasn't going I wasn't.

Once the sister had gone, a voice came through over the loudspeakers, a voice so loud that I, and all the other normal occupants of the airport lounge, jumped in our respective seats. Not The Most Laid-Back Guy Ever. He looked up slowly from where his eyes had been relaxed on the floor, as if the sound of the booming commands were a distant friend calling for him to please, look over here.

I got up to board the plane, fumbling ever so non-laid-backly with my bag. I was praying in my head, although it was more like chanting. *Let him sit next to me let him sit next to me.* An hour-and-a-half lesson on the ways of calm. Most likely, we would not speak, but his surfer-style contentment would flow through our shared armrest. Osmosis facilitated by flight attendants. I got up and stood in line. The man I envied most didn't make a move. What a good call.

WHEN HIS SISTER CAME BACK, she joined me in line. I saw her looking for The Most Laid-Back Guy Ever, but I also saw that he was leaning over in his seat and that she couldn't see him from where she was standing. If I hadn't known better, I would have said he was tying his shoelaces. I got out of line and hung back, watching The Most Laid-Back Saga Ever as it casually unfolded. There was neck craning, the look of a genuinely confused person, then a shrug that was so unruffled it must have been a genetic trait she shared with her brother. The sister got on the plane alone, probably assuming he had already done so. But the man I had spent this entire time watching, the one so clearly poised for a trip, an adventure, a new and stimulating experience that wouldn't faze him at all but which would simply sink into his aura—making him that much more remarkable at a dinner party—he stayed right where he was.

THERE'S AN OUT-OF-BODY EXPERIENCE YOU can have if the world is aligned just right. I, personally, had only ever been associated with its negative capabilities. It's the slowing that happens right before your car crashes. It's the clairvoyance that comes immediately upon having said the wrong thing. But as I stood against the wall of the airport lounge I was transported into the body of that man, the one sitting ever-so-loosely some ten feet away. I could both see him sitting there and at the same time see the coffee cart in his eyeline. Where usually I would have been put off by the look of stale beans trapped in a plastic jar above the coffee grinder, I now knew what I would see if I were The Most Laid-Back Guy Ever. I could smell the Brazilian field where the coffee was grown. I could remember the taste of the barista's first kiss. I could hear the innermost parts of the cash register whirling. I was attuned to everything and nothing; I was a part of the chair in which I sat, a part of the airport and a part of the air.

I wanted very much to keep standing there as the last boarding call was announced. The longer he sat, unmoving, the more it felt like we were in this together, like it was some sort of silent sit-in staged against the dictatorship that ruled John F. Kennedy airport. But just as I could see his form in front of me, legs planted wide, I could also see me, on time, walking into the office on Monday morning. It hardly counted as a prophecy. I would enter from the door on the far left of the room, holding my travel coffee cup. I would sit where I always sat and say what I always said.

I WAS SITTING IN THE middle of the plane, on the aisle. Just before the doors closed a woman seated behind me sprinted off, whispering hurriedly to the stewardess as she passed. Sister to The Most Laid-Back Guy Ever reappeared barely a minute later, leading him by the hand. They walked past me, and I stared up at them like a disciple at the foot of saints. We are never alone on planes. Some people want to be there and others feel trapped aboard a metal tube. Some are leaving loved ones, others returning to them. If we're lucky, or very well attuned, we catch ourselves reflected in the other passengers.

"It will be all right," she whispered to him as they passed. And I saw, just before he went out of sight, The Most Laid-Back Guy Ever press the heel of his right hand against his breastbone, push down, and sweep left to dislodge. ▯

stephanie bramson

STEPHANIE BRAMSON has a Bachelor's Degree in English/Creative Writing from Franklin and Marshall College, where her main focus was playwriting. Her plays have been performed in Pennsylvania, New York, Minnesota, and Florida. She has also written for Cracked.com under the pseudonym "Lauren Ipsum." Visit her website, www.stephaniebramson.com or her Tumblrs, iamlaurenipsum.tumblr.com and laurenipsumfiction.tumblr.com.

BECOMING JOHN DOE

I t figures that Ryan would leave his wallet home today, the day of his first job interview in six months. Maybe this is why no employers have contacted him before this one; they can psychically read him through his resume and know he's a screw-up, always late to everything. He curses himself for bragging about his punctuality in every cover letter.

Of course, he knows he's not always late. He reminds himself of this as he takes out his phone to Google the company's number. What company is it, again? Was it that startup looking for a web designer? The web designer looking for a personal assistant? One of those social media coordinator jobs that no one can define but every twenty-something with a Facebook page is qualified to do?

He looks back at his email. Oh, right. It's Target. Interviewing for a cashier and customer service rep position. At least if he could work in the electronics department, he'd be *close* to working in his field. Not that he particularly cared about computers in the first place. Ryan had put off going to college for as long as possible, working as a busser until he couldn't stand the thought of holding another dish rag. After matriculating, he majored in programming so he could get a job, unlike those loser English majors in his graduating class. Unfortunately for him, half the graduates of the last three years apparently made the same decision, and unlike him, they had internships and connections. Desperate for experience, he begged all of his friends and family to let him design their websites for a tiny fee. When that didn't work, he offered to do it for no charge. When that didn't work, he tried to pay them. Sadly, no one seemed to want a website. And now the best he can hope for is getting to buy a whole new wardrobe of red shirts and khaki pants for a new job at the fancier version of Walmart.

He knows no job is beneath him, especially now. And he wouldn't even mind working at Target if it weren't for his student loans. Ryan is in an abusive relationship with Sallie Mae, a woman who once seemed so sweet and giving, but then, after graduation, turned into a gold-digging monster. Sixty years ago, debt collectors broke your limbs if you failed to pay them back; Sallie Mae, one of the largest student loan agencies/portals to debtor's hell, just destroys your credit, maybe puts you in jail—Ryan isn't sure, but he's spent several sleepless nights wondering if borrowing from the Mob would have been less painful.

He tries to juggle his resume and his coffee cup and his phone as he dials Target's number while crossing the street.

"Hello? This is Ryan Fitzpatrick. I have an interview today and just wanted to let you know I'm going to be late—"

When the truck crashes into him, his coffee drenches his resume, and his phone flies under the wheel. By the time the pain kicks in, he's unconscious.

"I THINK HE'S WAKING UP," he hears. The bed feels unfamiliar. His arm is sore, and moving makes it worse. He hears voices and beeping noises. Hospital? He vaguely remembers seeing the front end of a truck awfully close to him, and the pain in his head and back lets him know exactly how well that turned out. He assumes he never made it to Target. *Guess that job's off the table.* Still, at least a hospital stay and recovery will give him an excuse to halt the job hunt. He's not looking forward to paying the copays for this visit.

Suddenly, his eyes open wide, hurting his head even more. Copays? He just turned twenty-six. He doesn't have insurance anymore. He planned on getting in on open enrollment, maybe looking into Medicaid, but like an idiot, he just never got around to it. He's already $100,000 in debt to Sallie Mae; what about this new bill? Would the nurses notice if he got up and left now?

"Glad to see you're awake," he hears from next to him. He turns to the side and sees a woman in a lab coat. "How are you feeling?"

"Okay, I guess," he answers, voice unsteady.

"You came in without any identification. What's your name?"

"R . . ." he starts. Wait a minute. Don't hospitals have to treat you even if you can't pay? And they can send all the bills they want to Ryan Fitzpatrick. John Doe, on the other hand . . .

". . . I don't know."

THEY SPEND DAYS INTERROGATING HIM, asking him to count to fifteen, name the president, remember six random words, draw a straight line. Within a week, he does all of the above perfectly. The only question he doesn't answer is his name. They search for missing persons, but nothing comes up. (Why would it? He calls home infrequently because his parents think he works twenty hours a day at some random bank, lives on his dwindling savings account with roommates from Craigslist, and is a generic unemployed single white male. Even on a milk carton, he'd be unremarkable). Finally, after two weeks of recovery from everything but imaginary amnesia, they let him go, against medical advice.

Go where? Home? He's almost out of rent money, not to mention money for food. And with Sallie Mae after him and no job to pay them off, it's only a matter of time before he loses that small amount of cash, too. Already, Sallie Mae's started calling him instead of just sending letters. Ryan Fitzpatrick is not keen on returning home. Neither is John Doe.

Suddenly, he remembers Eric Morgan. Eric Morgan, the weird kid from his senior seminar. You know how every group of friends has that one friend that nobody likes? That friend who won't stop talking and has an annoying voice, who always says the wrong thing and makes every gathering uncomfortable, whose existence is little more than a punch line for everyone else? That was Eric. He'd moved a few blocks from Ryan's apartment after graduation and asked Ryan to move in with him. Naturally, Ryan made his excuses, preferring life with strangers to living with Eric Morgan. But Eric's the type to post on Facebook when he has a bagel for breakfast, and he posted a picture of his key-holding door-knocker two months ago—thirty dollars on Etsy. Three weeks ago, he said he was going home for a few months. What job lets him go visit his parents for months at a time, Ryan didn't know. Telecommuting, probably—no sane company would ever want Eric in the office.

Without returning home, Ryan sneaks like a bank robber (or, more accurately, a preteen shoplifter) to Eric's vacant apartment. Feeling around the doorknocker for the trap that Eric photographed, he finds the key and opens the door. After several weeks of emptiness, the apartment has gathered some dust, but everything is immaculate, barely lived in—not anything like the Eric Ryan knew in school. The kitchen cupboards, however, are filled with canned food, ramen, and bottled water in preparation for the looming apocalypse—exactly like the Eric Ryan remembers. The electricity is still on, and Eric's bed is neatly made with fresh, albeit dusty, sheets. There is enough shampoo and soap in the shower for at least a month, plus what looks like every book Terry Pratchett ever wrote (may he rest in peace). Having heard rumors of XBox's tracking systems that rival Facebook's unconventional interpretation of the word "privacy," he doesn't dare touch Eric's console, which he's sure is loaded with Netflix and Hulu+, but his DVD player looks usable enough.

The one thing the apartment doesn't have is money. But then, even if it did, Ryan doesn't know if he could spend it. Breaking into Eric's apartment is one thing, stealing his food and shampoo and watching his DVDs is another thing, but taking his money . . . he can't even bring himself to ask his own parents for money. Everything else he'd take from

Eric would merely be borrowing from a friend without asking and without intention of returning. Robbery, somehow, is more intimate than sleeping in Eric's bed and using his towels.

Speaking of his parents, how long could John Doe let Mr. and Mrs. Fitzpatrick worry about their son? Before becoming a missing person, Ryan only called his parents once a week or so. It was exhausting, trying to fake a life. He wanted to be a man, living on his own without parental support, and his parents weren't wealthy. They didn't have the money they'd spend on him, if he let them. So he moved out, told them a bank had given him a salaried job, and hoped he'd be able to really live a version of the lie he'd created for them. They knew he was in debt, but he refused to let them pay it. Being John Doe would solve his debt problems, but what about his larger mission of keeping his parents sane? How long could he be John Doe before the world started to look for Ryan Fitzpatrick?

John Doe imagines Ryan Fitzpatrick's wallet on his old bed, packed with care like a first grader's lunch box—driver's license, social security card, credit cards, expired health insurance card, store cards, and a stream of business cards without a business, identifying him to the world as Ryan Fitzpatrick, a programmer without a program, a living person with no life. Forgetting his wallet gave him freedom, but would abandoning it make him a prisoner?

He tries to forget about all of this for the next few weeks. Every night, he sleeps in Eric's bed. Every morning, he uses Eric's shower. Every day, he reads Eric's books or watches Eric's movies, and every evening, he uses Eric's light switches. He dares not leave the apartment, lest he see his name and picture plastered everywhere as a missing person. Which would be worse, he wonders: to be found and returned to life as Ryan Fitzpatrick, racking up late fees and scrounging for employment anywhere that would keep him out of prison, or to never return and live off of Eric Morgan's tuna fish and canned beets forever? Which would be worse: to leave the apartment and get recognized from the news reports covering a missing millennial, or to leave the apartment and realize that no one was looking for him at all? That he was so generic and wrapped up in his own world that no one would ever think to find him?

Ryan Fitzpatrick hadn't left his mark on anything. Would John Doe?

He wonders how long it will be before Ryan Fitzpatrick is declared dead. Would his debts pass to his parents, or will they just go away forever? He wishes he could research this, but he doesn't want to be busted by a paranoid Internet search.

After three weeks, John Doe's reality becomes all-consuming. How much longer before Eric comes home? Will he die here, in Eric's living room? Without a license or a social security number, how will he ever get a job at all? Why does the modern world make it so hard to live off the grid? Could he steal a new identity, or borrow one? How do all of the criminals do it anyway? For all of his Netflix binges of crime procedurals, his street smarts are close to nonexistent.

One day, he searches in Eric's closet for the perfect hoodie to wear outside. Eric wore hoodies all the time in college, but Ryan never did. Maybe hiding his head would keep him from being recognized, and he could visit a library with no library card, or buy fruit with no spare change. As he pushes through flannel and fleece, he hears the door open. Shit. The living room is filled with dirty dishes and discarded DVD covers.

Silence fills the apartment for a moment. He hears the front door close and the hall closet door open. He prepares to run for the window when he sees Eric next to him, holding a broom like an ax. Stunned, Eric drops the broom.

"Ryan?"

"Shit . . . sorry, man, I didn't think you'd be back for months."

"What are you doing here?"

Ryan can't think of a good answer. Eric continues.

"Look, it doesn't matter, okay? I'm leaving."

"Going where?"

Eric pauses.

"You can't tell anyone this, okay?"

"Okay."

"I'm in an abusive relationship, and I have to get out of here. I have to get away from her. I'm moving to South America. New passport, new license—all of it. Eric Morgan won't exist anymore."

Ryan stares in confusion.

"You have all of that already?"

"I will soon. I'm getting ready to leave."

Ryan pauses.

"I can keep watch over everything, if you want," he tells Eric, slowly. "I can be you. I can be you with a haircut."

"You have your own life."

"I don't mind. I will give that up, for you. I will become Eric Morgan. Someone should be Eric Morgan. And I'll take care of that abusive girlfriend of yours, okay?"

Visibly confused, Eric nods. He gives John Doe his wallet, car keys, house keys, bank PIN, and bank cards, and like that, Ryan Fitzpatrick who became John Doe becomes Eric Morgan, who becomes some guy in South America.

"If Sally calls, run," the former Eric tells him as he walks out of his life.

THREE WEEKS LATER, RYAN RETURNS home from the food store, carrying several bags of perishable goods. He's taken Eric's resume and applied, as Eric, to every job he can find. He knows he'll find something soon.

As he puts the new milk in the fridge, his phone rings.

"Eric Morgan? This is Richard Brown from Sallie Mae." ▯

mina e holmes

MINA E. HOLMES is a Nebraskan writer and a recent graduate of the University of Nebraska–Lincoln. Her fiction has appeared in *Laurus*. She recently completed an internship with *Prairie Schooner*, and has served as copy editor of a literary anthology as well as a magazine centered on both youth culture and art. In addition to preparing for graduate school, Holmes is currently hard at work on a collection of short stories.

SMALL BUMP

There's a moment, a brief, unexpected moment, when I find myself gliding my hand across the flat expanse of my belly and imagining it: my stomach swelling with the heft of another life; cold gel and corny jokes while Sam holds my hand at the doctor's office; decorating a nursery with soft colors and cartoon animals. I picture a tiny person with Sam's warm brown eyes and my curly hair smiling up at me, all cuteness and giggles. A family, *our* family, happy and healthy.

A particularly loud snore from Sam snaps me back to reality. His warm body presses against mine, shoulder to hip, not so much out of affection as necessity; a twin bed is all we can afford. He shifts and whines, his face buried in his pillow and one arm hanging off the edge of the bed. I hope he won't try to reclaim the bicep that's probably bloodless after a night wedged under my head. I've gotten used to the cramped overlapping of his body and mine, the heat of his back on one side of me and the cool touch of the wall on the other. There's something comforting about the constancy. I move my hand, trying to ignore the proverbial bump in the road.

I know he's waking up when his breathing changes, but he's never functioning until the knuckles of his free hand knock on the slightly splintered wood of the floor. Almost a year of living together, and I still don't know why he does it. All our luck was exhausted after we met each other.

"Mornin'," he groans, turning his head to look at me. He tugs his trapped arm, and I lift up just enough for him to wriggle it out from under my head. It lands softly on my abdomen, like it would on any other lazy Sunday morning: the backs of his fingers grazing the wall, heavy forearm weighing me down. Then he remembers, like I did, that my belly isn't just mine anymore, and he pulls his hand away.

OVER THE BREAKFAST TABLE, WHICH is really a rescued coffee table that we sit on the floor to use, Sam and I take turns looking at each other from the corner of our eyes. It's stupid, really, that we both know the other is aware of our staring but can't stop trying to take a peek. He looks for a few seconds, then I chase his gaze away, and our roles reverse. The sound of our metal spoons pushing off-brand Froot Loops around in their Styrofoam bowls is the loudest thing in the room, aside from the staccato clicking and thudding of the radiator in the corner.

Six weeks. The doctor told us I'd been carrying it for six weeks already.

When I'm not chomping on my cereal, my jaw is working, stress grinding my teeth into nubs. My shoulders are pinched at the base of my neck, and I know I won't be able to release my hand's death-grip around the spoon until we talk. My throat starts to feel like an erupting geyser of stomach acid and tears, but I choke it down.

"What are we gonna do?" I wince at the sound of him sliding his half-empty bowl onto the table. He sighs and leans forward, elbows resting on his knees.

"We'll do whatever you want, Amelia." He never calls me Amelia.

"I want your opinion, *Samuel*. Wouldn't ask if I didn't." I can't control the sharpness of my voice. If I didn't know him so well, I'd mistake his noncommittal shrug for indifference.

"It's your body."

"But it's *our* future."

"You think I don't know that?"

"This is a big deal. The biggest deal."

"And I'll support you in your choice."

"So you want a baby? You know that's what we're discussing, right? A baby, not a haircut."

"I love you, Ames." And he does, I know, but I wish he didn't look so goddamn miserable about it.

"So what the hell are we going to do?"

"We can't afford a baby." He says it slowly, enunciating each word, waiting for them to sink in.

"I know," I say, picking at the cheap carpet. The pale blue paint on the walls has been chipped to hell since before we moved in, and we can't go more than a month without some sort of leak or break. We hung posters over the peepholes that were drilled into the bathroom walls before we moved in because caulk wasn't in the budget. By the end of each month, enough food for both of us means scrounging around, shuffling money between accounts. How the hell would we buy formula?

"So," he says, "what about alternatives?"

"Adoption?" Even as I say it, it doesn't feel right, but Sam doesn't notice my hesitation. He thinks on it while I pull my lip between my teeth waiting for an answer. His face brightens.

"That'd be cool, right? Like, maybe our kid gets adopted by millionaires and grows up filthy rich. Might even do water polo and shit." When *that* smile takes over his face, the cute but sort of dopey one that brings out his boyishness, a lump forms in my throat.

I want to bask in the contagiousness of his optimism, to smile at him like he's smiling at me, but I can't. My mind flits to my cousin Jenny, who bounced from bad foster homes to worse ones for years before landing with my aunt and uncle. I remember vague news stories about parentless children being used and abused by the people paid to care for them. Worse, I learned in a psych course I took that black kids are even less likely to get adopted. The more elaborate part of my brain considers Little Orphan Annie and Miss Hannigan, Pip and Mrs. Joe, Harry Potter and the Dursleys—and our kid probably won't be saved by magic or a benevolent bene-factor. I imagine him being scared and alone, convinced that I didn't want him. But I do. I do want a kid. Just not yet.

When I don't respond, Sam goes on, dreaming up all the things our kid could have, but probably won't. I can't stop him at first. And then I remember how even the best case scenario requires about thirty more weeks of escalating bodily pains and cravings and sacrifices and strangers touching me without permission.

In bed it was easy to picture an easy pregnancy. I wasn't imagining the looks I'd get walking in my cap and gown at graduation, my stomach beating me to my diploma. Now, instead of picturing me and Sam at an ultrasound, I'm thinking of sitting down two sets of perpetually disappointed parents to tell them that they're about to be upgraded to perpetually disappointed grandparents. There's no room in our apartment for a nursery, and, somehow, picturing a thrifted crib wedged into the corner of our cramped bedroom is harder for me to romanticize.

My fantasy of keeping our brown-eyed, curly-haired baby is collapsing under the weight of dollar signs, but I still can't wrap my head around the idea of making something so small and familiar, and leaving it with strangers.

"Stop it, please."

He blinks at me, furrowing his brow, then looks away.

"Look, I'm not sure that I can do this." His Adam's apple bobs slowly, eyes pasted on the wilting wildflowers jammed into a glass bottle on the table.

"Oh."

"I'm not ready for this, Sam." My hands shake as I tell him, so I wrap them around my knees. It doesn't help. "I'm sorry, but I can't."

When he stands up, I'm almost afraid that he'll leave, that I've fucked it all up. He doesn't. He just comes around the table, and holds out both hands until I let him pull me into the tightest hug he can manage without injury.

I MAKE THE APPOINTMENT ON Monday morning. Sam isn't home to hold my shaking hands, so I alternate between shoving the free one in my pocket and biting jagged nails. The assistant on the phone is polite and accommodating, and we set up a time with the doctor. Friday afternoon, just after my Economics test.

As I get ready for class, I stand before the mirror, shirtless, my belly expanded as far as it can go. It makes me look, and feel, like Violet Beauregarde.

▯

I TUG AT THE SCARF around my neck, dreading the walk to campus. Just like every other day, I walk past the long lines of apartment buildings like ours, all uniform and gray, slightly less beaten up on the outside than on the inside. They somehow still blend easily with the town homes, which aren't really so different from the small houses that line the next few blocks. Across the street is the park that I usually cut through to shave a few minutes. Small children in coats and hats race around the dying grass, laughing and playing. Their mothers, probably stay-at-home moms, all wear these lazy smiles and talk about recipes or diapers or whatever else they talk about.

I don't cut through the park today. Instead, I let my combat boots crunch loudly through the unraked edge of grass lining the street.

▯

LEAH IS THE FIRST PERSON besides Sam to find out. We've been best friends since high school, and it's a little unsettling to think that there's something so big I haven't already told her about. She's been the steadiest fixture of the last seven years of my life; she's gotten me through awful relationships, worse haircuts, and a particularly bad semester of Calculus, but I need her now more than ever.

I ask her to meet me for lunch on campus. Greasy Chinese food is always our meal of choice. We get takeout containers and park ourselves on a bench in the union. I sit facing her, my legs curled on either side of the bench, while she crosses her legs and angles toward me. Even though I see her every day, I'm a little surprised when I look at Leah this time. It's like I'd forgotten that she'd chopped her hair into a pixie cut last month. Her cheeks have thinned out with age and there's a grace, a subtle confidence I think, that she definitely didn't have back then. It's crazy, really, how grown-up she looks after seven years. It's crazier to think that I probably look just as grown-up, but don't feel it at all.

"I have news," I say.

"Good or bad?"

"I'm pregnant." She drops her fork into her container and freezes.

"Really?"

"And I'm getting rid of it."

"Shit, Mel. Like, getting rid of it, or *getting rid of it*?" Her tone isn't sharp or judgmental. It never is. Talking to Leah isn't like speaking to my mother or one of my four perfect, married sisters. Not once, not since we were fourteen years old, has she ever made me feel judged.

"I set up an appointment this morning."

I remember why she's my best friend when she doesn't ask why. She just nods once, slowly blinking her green eyes at me. When we were younger, she and I would set up picture-perfect scenarios of being married at twenty-five with babies and careers and social lives that somehow miraculously worked well together. We thought we could have it all.

"You've already talked to Sam, I take it?"

"He's not thrilled, but he gets it." I feel that same guilt coming back. What if he doesn't get it?

She puts her hand over mine, squeezing when I tell her about my appointment. It's almost like asking her to be a bridesmaid when I ask her to come with me to my abortion. I'm not sure how, but I completely bypass the misty-eyed crying stage and go straight into blubbering mess. They're my people, Sam and Leah, and it's a minor relief to know I'll have them both when the time comes.

IT'S ON TUESDAY NIGHT WHEN I'm propped up on my pillow in bed and biting my nails that I finally ask. Sam just crawled in beside me, groaned about some rude customer accosting him at the hardware store, kissed my bare shoulder, and turned over to go to sleep.

"Am I a heartless bitch?"

There's a low rumble beside me, a throaty laugh lost in Sam's pillow, before he turns to look up at me. I don't want to be distracted by how flattering the soft moonlight is on his strong jaw and dark skin, but I still smooth my hand along his scruffy face. He's really handsome when he laughs. He's handsome and he's also kind, one of the kindest people I've ever met, but I'm not ready to see his charming, goofy features on our baby. I would do almost anything for Sam, but I can't do this. When he realizes I'm not joking his face falls. He pushes himself up to my level, sits on his heels, and sighs.

4️⃣

"Amelia, babe, you aren't a heartless bitch."

"This is the most selfish thing I've ever done."

"Or the smartest."

"It's selfish, Sam. *I'm* selfish."

"Because you don't want to spend the rest of your life wondering who you could've been if you didn't have a kid before you were ready? That's not selfish."

"I'm choosing myself, Sam. I'm choosing myself over this baby because I'm not ready for our lives to change."

"Me neither, Ames, but they're changing. One way or another."

I'm not ready. We aren't ready. When Sam had the flu he puked all over the floor and I mopped it up with old magazines. We've strategically avoided the stain ever since. I can't get up at four a.m. to change a diaper—not because I value my sleep, but because I'm underqualified to change diapers. As much as I love Sam, he's still ridiculously messy and a little gross. If the perpetual mustard stain outlining the gaping hole on the thigh of his favorite boxers is any indication, then our kid would probably always look a little homeless. We shouldn't be parents yet. We *can't* be parents right now, and I'm not ready to share my body like this for eight more months. It's invasive and scary and maybe even dangerous.

"Why is this so hard?"

"It's hard because it matters, I think." He's right. It matters.

WHEN MY MOTHER CALLS, I'M tempted to ignore it. I shouldn't be surprised, since she scheduled in weekly calls with my sisters and me, a one-on-one chat for each weekday, and cross-checked them with our availability. It's Wednesday, and she asks me somewhere north of twenty questions without pausing for answers. She goes on and on about each of my sisters' accomplishments—potty training, new puppy, big promotion, ranch-style house on the edge of the burbs— but when she mentions how much they missed me on the last family group call, I almost call bullshit. If anything, Anna and Amanda were too distracted by their own mindless chatter to notice that my near-silence and sighing were absent; if Alexa or Alicia missed me, it's probably because I've forgotten to return something that they insisted I borrow. Being in the same room as all of them is like joining in on a sorority brunch, but the small age gap between me and each of my sisters does nothing to cushion the fact that I'm never really invited.

Like always she puts Dad on to offer me money—if I need it—then we all pretend that his generosity isn't contingent upon me cutting ties with Sam. It doesn't phase me when Dad not-so-subtly asks whether Sam's still working the same position at the hardware store. God forbid a college student keep a menial job for more than a year, even if it pays half the bills. It's only years of practice that allow me to make noncommittal noises of assent at exactly the right moments without actually listening to my parents.

Really, I spend the entire call reasoning with myself that I'm not *actually* nauseous. My mother ticks away the time while I curl my hand over my mouth and fiddle with the receiver to make sure she won't hear me gag.

I can't bring myself to tell her today that I'm pregnant when, in two days' time, I won't be.

LEAH AND I SPEND THURSDAY cutting our classes to sit on a park bench in too-cold weather. We talk about her internship, my ridiculous family, our senior year of high school. When we start shivering too hard, we hop on the campus bus and ride it to the hardware store where Sam works. He kisses me while Leah and his coworkers wolf-whistle, like we don't have a care in the world.

ON FRIDAY, SAM AND LEAH walk me into the clinic, each holding one of my hands until my name is called and I go on alone. There isn't blood lining the clinic walls, and I don't faint at the sight of invasive surgical tools. The stirrups are cold and the doctor impersonal, but the nurse stays to hold my hand when I ask. It doesn't hurt as much as I thought it would. When it's over, I take my time slipping back into my clothes, smoothing my hand over my still puffed-out belly. I feel lighter, even if it's just dizziness, and Sam and Leah are there when the doctor releases me, like always, supporting me.

We catch a bus to get home. Leah slides into the window seat, and I sit next to her. Even though there are tons of open spots, Sam stands in the aisle next to me. Neither of them say a word, and I'm grateful. According to the doctor, I'm a couple prescriptions away from putting all of this behind me. I run my hand along the small bump of my belly, virtually unchanged in the last few hours, still a barely bloated version of what it was six weeks ago. Nobody knew besides Sam and Leah. No one will accidentally ask about cravings or morning sickness or potential preschool options. My stomach won't be groped or petted by strangers. In eight months, I'll be a lot of things, but still not a mother. It's almost like none of this ever happened, but I'll always know it did.

I wasn't ready, and neither was Sam. This whole process feels like pressing pause. Life was moving too quickly, our baby growing too quickly, and I had to put it on hold. It's stupid, I know, but part of me imagines my baby, this baby, waiting patiently inside some dormant part of my body for me to be ready. Not dead, waiting.   ▢

▶ I CAN'T BRING
MYSELF TO TELL
HER TODAY THAT
I'M PREGNANT
WHEN IN TWO
DAYS' TIME,
I WON'T BE.

jared shaffer

JARED SHAFFER'S stories have appeared in *Cellar Door, Red Cedar Review,* and *West Trade Review.* He received an English degree from the University of North Carolina at Chapel Hill, where he won the George B. Wynne and Max Steele Awards for Fiction. He works in publishing in New York.

USE
WITHOUT
PITY

Even though Mina and I call in sick half an hour apart, our boss at the movie theater accepts both our excuses, grunting and mumbling a curse. His drinking has reappeared, triggering what I call "the lean": he's more lenient with us but also more apt to fall over. I pick Mina up from her apartment. The morning is bright, my car's leather seats are burning, and the slow breeze that hits us at stoplights feels like it can freeze time.

We drive out to a meadow that seems to belong to no one. I just built this potato launcher with the help of a neighbor who claimed it can decapitate an elk at thirty yards. On the side of it, he wrote "use without pity" in black marker. Mina and I are taking Friday off to try the thing out. I am waging war against our platonic relationship.

This date worries me because Mina likes ideas more than what they unfold to be. When employees get together for a pre-release viewing, she never stays for more than the first half because she thinks it's beat-up that the rest of the movie steps in and tells you how to think about its beginning.

During last week's screening she put her hand on my thigh, but that could've been a mistake at first, as my pants were made of the same itchy cloth as the theater's armrests. I fit my hand over hers and squeezed it with some gusto, but she didn't flinch, didn't bat an eye. We stayed that way—our hands forming a miniature, sweating greenhouse—until she left halfway through.

I unfurl a checkered wool blanket onto the grass, and we sit. In front of us, next to a picnic basket full of russet potatoes, is the launcher. It's a few plastic pipes, held together with neon yellow cement that's dried and stained along the cracks where the pipes connect, and a push-button grill igniter. Past the launcher is more field, a basketball court that has no rims attached to its backboards, and a line of trees at least a hundred yards from us.

This is the summer before things start to change. Next year, Mina will marry a lawyer who can tie his tie in more ways than I can cook an egg. Next year, I'll move back in with my parents, who will tell me they always saw it coming. This summer, though, when I ask Mina out, is before all that. This summer, Mina still eats with her mouth open and wears jean shorts that stick to her thighs like Gorilla Glue. I don't owe the world a thing and the cigarette packs I find in between theater seats feel like out-of-season stocking stuffers.

Right now, we pass back and forth a plastic bottle of champagne and a tub of popcorn I stole from work last night. We compare hand sizes, and she shoves me onto the dead grass and sits on top of me. She leans in close, her lips buttery from the popcorn. Then she whispers something I can't make out, something that sounds delicate and sultry.

"What?" I say.

She says, "Let's fire this potato launcher already."

I'm not sure if that's what she said the first time. Hairspray goes in one end of the PVC pipe and the potato in the other. I pull the trigger and the potato jumps out of the barrel, arcing over the basketball court and dropping into the woods in just a few seconds. I hoot and she laughs.

Before I can offer her the second shot, she walks out into the field, carrying the champagne bottle at her side, its neck pinched between her fingertips. The bottle bounces lightly against her thigh. Out there, the grass is as tall as her shins. After about twenty yards, she turns around, snaps her body to attention, and balances the bottle on her head. "You know that story of the kid whose dad shoots an apple off his head?" she says.

"You can't aim this thing."

"You can. Shoot the bottle off my head."

"It was a fable. None of that actually happened."

"His dad's arrow split the apple perfectly. Are you afraid of missing? Are you afraid of me?"

For a moment, I imagine Mina being here before: same place, same dare, different man. I imagine him saying no, laying the launcher at her feet. Good for him. There's comfort in a life lived in circles and its careful, sloping lines. But I'm betting that Mina is looking for someone who will tell her yes instead of no. Someone who can see things through. Someone who will watch the second half of a movie with her.

Out in the field, with grass covering up her feet and part of her legs, she seems immobile. She is smiling as though a machine is tugging at her mouth from both sides. I load the launcher and, aiming with one eye open and the other closed, let the potato go. ▯

theresa buchta

THERESA BUCHTA received her Bachelor's Degree in English Literature with a concentration in Creative Writing from Hofstra University in 2015. She grew up in Connecticut and is currently completing a Master's of Arts degree in Writing at Columbia University. She lives in New York City. This is her first publication.

VICTORIA

ictoria said goodbye to her mother, who was paying bills at the kitchen table. The yellow glow from the hanging lamp dispersed over the room. Dawn was a little while away, and the neighbor's multi-colored Christmas lights shone through the window. It was Sunday, Victoria's day off, and she had no reason to be awake at this hour, but her mother sat in her stiff-backed chair drinking tea and did not question it.

She did nothing to disguise her departure, jingling the keys and asking if her mother had to use the car that day. She already knew the answer. There was a list of chores tacked up on the fridge and none of them involved leaving the house. There was also a reminder to call the lawyer. Clutter, papers and letters, and her brothers' schoolwork swamped the couch and kitchen counters.

She poured tea into a travel mug. Henry said once they reached Virginia it wouldn't be long before she started drinking coffee; everything was deeper there, he said. More intense. She didn't know what that meant but she hated the chalky, bitter taste of coffee.

Her mother waved her off. "It's Sunday. Don't worry about me, go have some fun," she said, as if she *knew*, and was all but inviting Victoria to take the plunge.

She emptied the dishwasher and bundled a load of clothes into the laundry before she left. Gym shorts and T-shirts that belonged to her little brothers. None of them hers. She wondered if her mother had noticed. Henry had driven by on Friday to pick up her suitcase. All she had was a small paper bag of belongings.

"Are you sure you don't need me to do anything else?"

"Don't worry about me, honey," she said, copying down numbers from a checkbook. "You deserve a little fun. Isn't there a boy?" she asked, putting down her pen and looking up over the rim of her glasses.

"Yes," Victoria said softly.

The air bit her cheeks, cold cutting through her jacket. The sun turned yellow on the snow. Across the street, a hill dipped down into a wide field. Victoria had lived here since she was born. For the first ten years of her life, her world had been narrowed into the street and the hill and the school down the road. Winters were spent on her father's old-fashioned wooden sled with the nails that poked out the bottom; four or five children would pile on top of the two-person toboggan, the logic being that more weight made you fly faster down the slope. There'd been ten or eleven children on the street, but her favorite had been the Watson girls. The twins and their older sister. She'd been closer to the twins, two solemn redheads with mischievous intentions. The older sister ran away in high school with a college boy and came back pregnant, unmarried, and beaming. It was all very scandalous at the time. Victoria had caught a glimpse of her strolling her baby down the street that summer. The older girl hadn't looked like the miserable slut everyone accused her of being. Victoria had blushed and felt warmth in her belly. A coil of repulsion—no, embarrassment, like she should have disapproved but instead felt a strange attraction to the girl's soft, motherly limbs and the red-faced wrinkly creature in the carriage.

She gave no thought to how the girl had gotten this way, the man-boy who'd impregnated her. He didn't stay in the Watsons' lives. There were rumors that he mailed a check every month from California, or Alaska, or Canada sometimes. Realms far outside Victoria's consciousness. She grew older but her curiosity lingered, the strange sort of awe she had of the girl's pleasure. She'd gone away and disappeared and something had happened in the interim. Victoria wondered about that. It never quite left her.

Other things began to change. Victoria's father didn't last in the marriage to her mother. Two years ago he'd packed his bags and boxes and told her mother he'd go after her for everything she had, for being a heinous, controlling bitch all those years, cutting his hours short at the bar, duping him into having kids, raiding the cash box—with his permission, of course, but that detail seemed to escape him by the time the court date rolled around.

After he left they discovered the mortgage hadn't been paid in two years. The bar's business had crashed. They were bankrupt. Her mother had to borrow money from her own parents to pay off the debt. The judge had ruled in favor of a restraining order against her father. Now all that was left were the final court proceedings and negotiations between their lawyers. It all looked to be in her mother's favor. Everything was finally settling down.

Except Victoria's father had stopped paying her university tuition along with the mortgage and she'd had to come home to be with her mother and brothers. She applied for a job as a bank teller downtown, which was ironic, all things considered. She worked long hours, completing menial tasks beyond answering phone calls and depositing checks, things like arranging candies in little dishes and ordering mass shipments of pens. She did the grocery shopping and cooked dinner, which could be fun sometimes when her brothers helped and they experimented with exotic recipes. She spent a lot of time ignoring the messages on the answering machine that were threats from her father, and listening to her mother cry when everyone was out of the room and she thought they couldn't hear her.

She didn't hate her family, none of them, she swore it, even her father, who was pathetic and manipulative but not hate-worthy. She didn't want to leave any of them for good; she'd told Henry she'd write a note to them when they reached Virginia, explain where she was and not to worry, and maybe even send money if she was able. He'd been very good-natured about it—he was a very good-natured man— but something about the way he chuckled a little made her think he didn't believe she would actually do it.

There was a farm in Virginia that some of his friends had bought after college. They grew the usual crops and also had a covert operation in one of the greenhouses out back, and she'd frowned a little at that when he told her, and he'd said, "*You know*," and she was pleased to realize she was worldly enough that she did know. He painted a picture of green hills rolling lazily into the distance. They farmed and it was good work, solid work, but not work that broke you. They drank iced tea and beer and at night they lounged under the stars until the stars became their reality and the tether they had to the earth was gone.

It was there, he'd promised, that she would be given freedom to breathe and relax and come face to face with herself and figure things out.

She turned out of the driveway and drove an hour to the airport, through the small quiet morning snuffles of town— joggers and errand runners and children with paper bags full of bagels—and then onto the highway. She turned the nose of the car south, toward the city.

Henry said he was waiting for her at the terminal. She passed through security with her brown paper bag. The linoleum floor was cold beneath her bare feet and she was jumpy through the security gate. The guard gestured her through with a brusque, sharp edge and she gathered her belongings, trying not to fumble or flinch beneath the gaze of the cop that lurked at the end of the conveyor belt. As if she was guilty of something.

She held her bag to her chest and thought that she'd feel better once Henry—large, calm, stoic Henry—was by her side. She tucked a strand of hair behind her ear and hoped no one would recognize her. The airport wasn't so far from home and it was vacation soon, when people went on winter holidays.

Gate twenty-two. She counted her way up from the fourteenth terminal. It was a small airline, the only one Henry could find flying to Virginia on a Sunday. They could go

another day, she'd suggested, but he was nothing if not deter-
mined. He was thoughtful, though a little broody at times,
and when she asked what the matter was, he said he was worried about his friends on the farm—the business end of
things, money, produce, the organization of Saturday
morning farmers markets. And she dropped it then, charmed
that he cared so much.

Henry splurged on her with flowers and books he liked
and an iPod with a built-in playlist he'd designed for her. He
treated her to concerts of people she'd never even heard of,
though she recognized some of their songs from the radio,
and treated her to candlelit dinners at restaurants with cloth
napkins and a wide variety of wines, and when she expressed
concern at the cost he laughed and explained that he had
his inheritance and besides, he only had himself to take care
of—and her too, now. He'd been the one to buy her the
plane ticket.

When she reached the correct terminal it was nearly
deserted. It was eight o' clock in the morning. Boarding was
about to begin. Henry stood at the wide glass windows that
peered out at the runway, his back to her, but she did not see
him so much as she saw through him. She came up behind
him. He did not sense her at first. She didn't alert him to her
presence, just stared out the window with him. The runway
splayed out at her feet, and at its point was the wide sky,
boxed in only by the edge of the glass pane, and at its height
were the limits of the world, or the limits of this world.

Funny, she remembered an oath she had sworn to herself
at the start of this, the night she watched her father walk out
on them. She'd promised to remain angry, to not go soft
toward him, and to stand by her mother's side. But that was

before she was tired and things were hard. She wanted to try, at least, for a different kind of life, and Henry had the vision and the means to make that possible. Henry would carry her out of this place; he would break the boundaries of her own small mind. She was convinced somewhere deep down in her bones—and she was starting to believe maybe it was something like intuition—that Henry could save her.

The boarding call came. People moved, families with children and a group of soldiers huddled in a solemn mass. Henry stroked her arm in delight, his touch hot and clammy from the perspiration of the coffee cup that had been in his hand. People swelled around them, threatening to sweep them away like a tidal wave, and she balked at their haste. She had expected more time at the terminal, a few more minutes to stare at the blue sky and adjust herself to the reality of departure. "Where's your boarding pass?" Henry asked.

"It's in my pocket," she said, half in a trance, and he pulled it out for her.

The crowd jostled and moved forward. A child's lollipop got stuck to her pant-leg. Henry led her by the hand and she let him, up to a certain point. She dawdled, fiddled with her bag, until they were last in line.

The flight attendant made the second to last call, and then, a few minutes later, the final boarding summons. Henry went ahead, handed his pass to the attendant. She checked it with a red laser beam and signaled him through. He lingered at the mouth of the tunnel that would lead to the plane's round gut. "Victoria," he said. "Vicky."

Her mouth was paste. The tunnel was a cavernous beast and Henry its teeth. She needed more time. Another hour or day. She saw the planes taking off through the window. They should have made noise, they should have been howling with the wind created by their engines. The appropriate departure, a dramatic farewell; like permission, like the universe itself was propelling her forward.

But the gate was still and silent. She couldn't hear Henry anymore, though his mouth gaped open and flapped around. He made a gesture as if to go to her but her body moved of its own accord and jerked away. If she let him touch her he'd snap her up; but if she didn't go the universe would swallow her whole. Indecision and anticipation lingered in her, were easier, more sure and solid.

She had a thought. Her luggage was on that plane. Stacked in with the rest, black and unidentifiable except for her initials on a tag. It would fly to Virginia. She couldn't stop that from happening. No flagging down the plane. It would touch down and in a way she would touch down with it, and in her heart she would carry the secret of a bag in Virginia that belonged to her.

She would be here, real, in the flesh, breathing. Maybe, if she focused on that, the sound of the world would become clear again.   ◻

▶ SHE'D PROMISED TO REMAIN ANGRY, TO NOT GO SOFT TOWARD HIM, AND TO STAND BY HER MOTHER'S SIDE. BUT THAT WAS BEFORE SHE WAS TIRED AND THINGS WERE HARD.

angus mclinn

ANGUS McLINN graduated from Macalester College in 2012 with a degree in Creative Writing and German Studies. He is currently an MFA candidate and Teaching Fellow at Long Island University Brooklyn. Additionally, he is an editor at *Visceral Brooklyn*, Long Island University's online literary journal. His poetry and fiction have appeared in *Those That This*, *Visceral Brooklyn*, *Tempered Magazine*, *Tiger Train Magazine*, *Marco Polo Arts Magazine*, *2013 Saint Paul Almanac*, and elsewhere. His articles have been featured in the *Wisconsin State Journal*, *Capital Times*, *Local Sounds Magazine*, and *Liberator Magazine*. He is the author of the fiction chapbook *Your Heart Really Does Explode* (Cloud City Press, 2012).

BABY TEETH

Cold-sweat, liquor-throat mornings weren't the same after that. At first, sleeping in back of the Weirdsmobile had filled my bones with a light sort of outlaw freedom, like the grooves of the truck bed that dug into my back and neck through my sleeping bag were just growing pains on the way to something bigger than anyone had ever known before. Now when I woke up in the morning, my bones hurt. Something deep under the skin and inside the vertebrae had frozen tight. If I could just press on it hard enough, it would pop and crack and shoot cool relief circulating through my muscles and nerves, but I could never get the right angle, never get behind myself the exact right way to let it all loose. The saltiness of our diet—ramen, baked beans, food court Chinese food, stuff like that—was making my blood flow thin and sharp, like the crystals had somehow gotten stuck in the cells and were scraping the walls of my veins. The icicle lights that lit our tented-over truck bed didn't make me laugh or smile the way they used to.

Frank didn't ask me if I wanted to talk about it the morning after Andy Pfeiffer—that was the name of the kid who fell off the Log Chute—died. He just hooked up the car battery to the electric kettle and the hot plate like always and started fixing morning chow. Today it was Easy Mac mixed with packets of water-packed albacore tuna. Once we each had a steaming bowl of noodles in front of us and Frank had taken some Taco Bell sporks out of the plastic bag we kept utensils in, I reached into the foot of my sleeping bag and pulled out one of the beers I kept down there to keep them from exploding during the freezing Minnesota nights.

"That's a road you don't want to go down yet, Mike," Frank said without looking up from his food, his words pushing through the steam from his bowl, thick and bullish.

The air hissed warm with condensation as I popped the tab on the can. The sick–sweet life smell of fermentation filled the tent and my nostrils then the back of my throat as I took a long sip. "What's that about, Frank?" I asked him. "You've never cared about me drinking before. Shit, you're having a beer right now," I said, pointing to the can sitting on the truck bed by his knee.

Frank ate like an old man. He took another bite of his fish and noodles and chewed it long and slow, working the muscles under the gray hair on his temples like it was something to think about, grumbling deep in his throat as he swallowed. "That's because you never had a reason for it before," he said and reached into the plastic bag to root around for a packet of Chinese hot sauce.

The hair on the back of my neck vibrated, not at all from the cold, and my heart woke up. I took another long sip of beer and let it thicken the roof of my mouth, warm and full. "What the fuck is that supposed to mean?" I asked. I'd never told him how I got to where I was. Somehow living in the Weirdsmobile felt safer if he didn't know about my life back in Wisconsin before I'd met him on the side of the highway and we'd gone to work for Maggie at Camp Snoopy. The soccer team and the broken bones, the pills and the pinched-skin humiliation of my dad shaving my head, quitting rehab, Carly. Carly, who was probably waking up right now, about to go to school and sit with Ryan Sakko in study hall, where he'd horse around with her and brush his palm across her tit only kind-of-on-purpose until the librarian told him to cut it out or go to the office.

Frank ripped open the Chinese hot sauce with his teeth and spit out the corner of the plastic packet. He squirted it onto his noodles—thick and red, oxygenated blood on a scraped knee. "It means that you don't look old enough to have been Army, and you don't look tough enough to have been Navy, so I'd wager that kid who fell off the Log Chute was the first person you've ever watched die," he said.

The angry jolt of the adrenaline gave out all of a sudden, a firecracker with too short a fuse that exploded in my hand and rang in my ears and I was nauseous and he was right. My voice cracked when I said his name. "Andy Pfeiffer."

"Who now?" Frank asked, stirring the Chinese hot sauce into his noodles and watching them turn pink.

"The kid who died, his name was Andy Pfeiffer," I said.

Frank looked at me, very sorry. More sorry than I'd ever seen anybody, even Mom as she'd watched Dad throw me into the backseat of the car by the shoulder the day they sent me to Lawson.

"You don't want to do that, Mike," Frank said. He took a long sip out of his can and it hit the truck bed thin and metallic, empty. "You don't want to learn their names."

📱

THE REGULAR CREW WAS ABOUT fifteen or twenty people. It was a pretty even split between community college kids and older guys who looked like peewee hockey coaches, short and square with tool-belt-leather faces and big ears. Me and Frank were crunched up in the corner next to the microwave and a skinny rock-and-roll-looking kid named Brogan. Even with so many people in it, the room was too cold, so everybody was still wearing their coats.

Maggie stood up front, her thick hair pulled back tight in a ponytail and steam from her coffee cup framing her chin. "Well, I suppose I should start this off by making sure that everybody's heard about what happened," she said. "Yesterday there was an incident on the Log Chute. A guest, a little boy named Andy Pfeiffer, panicked and managed to get himself out of the car just before the final drop. Unfortunately, this resulted in him falling to his death. Obviously, the whole Camp Snoopy family is devastated."

Everyone in the small room was shifting from one foot to the other, and the collective sound of their coats on each other's shoulders and backs caused a high-pitched sort of friction that got under your skin and just behind your forehead. Nobody said anything. There really wasn't much else to say.

The rest was the part I didn't really hear. Something about an investigation, mandatory grief counseling. The sweat seemed to come faster and faster and the smell from the microwave had gotten through my nose to the back of my throat and I could taste it. I wanted to vomit, but if I did, it would just be beer and cheese sauce and tuna, and it seemed like that would just make me vomit more, until the whole room was filled with it and I was empty and stretched across the floor, my insides out, just like Andy.

Frank put a paw on my shoulder and snapped me out of it. The meeting was over and everyone was muttering and shuffling out the door. "This one's trying to talk to you," he said, jerking a thumb at Brogan.

"Hey, man," Brogan said. His voice was a thick mix of Coon Rapids and California, equal parts nasal and lazy. "That was pretty heavy. Were you there? Like, when it happened?"

"Yeah, I was there," I said. I didn't know why, but it pissed me off that he'd even ask, like I would be standing here looking like shit and feeling this way if I hadn't seen it happen.

"Wow, must have been rough. I didn't even have to come in yesterday. Well, man, you and your dad are in my group for the counseling thing this weekend. You guys want a ride?" he said.

I looked at Brogan, blank, and wondered how he knew my dad. Frank laughed, but for once it was soft around the edges, and he made like he was going to muss my hair, although it still hadn't really grown back from when my real dad shaved my head, so it was more like a scrape. "I'd be a lot more disappointed than I am right now if this was my boy," he said.

Brogan ran a hand across the back of his head and left it there too long, pulling his hair. "Oh, sorry, I just figured since you guys got here at the same time and are always hanging out . . ." he said.

"Oh yeah . . . no. Frank is just a family friend," I said. I shot a look over at Frank, who was grinning over my shoulder. He flashed his eyes wide at me.

"Yeah, I knew his dad in the war. He sent him up here for the season to do some honest work. He was having girl problems at home," Frank said, finishing in a stage whisper. The waves of panic in my back and lungs had slowed down but were still buzzing steadily at the edge of my nerves and my stomach was still rotten. I didn't have enough feelings left to be pissed at Frank for being an asshole, so I let out an embarrassed laugh and hoped that he would leave it at that.

Brogan opened his mouth and I thought he might ask what war Frank was in, but then he stopped and just smiled. Brogan smiled like he smiled all the time, like smiling was just the kind of thing you did when you were talking to people or going to work or offering somebody a ride to grief counseling. "Well, either way I could give you fellas a lift if you want. Camp Snoopy family sticks together and all that, right?" he said. My guts rotted a little more.

"Yeah, cool," I said. "We'll meet you in the west lot out front of Nordstrom."

"Right on, guys, I'll see you Saturday," Brogan said, then he ducked out the door and into the hallway to the main floor.

Frank got a look on his face like he was about to say something else stupid, but the rot was spreading from my stomach going upward and I knew I had to get out of there. I lunged out the door and down the hall to the employee bathroom and vomited. When I stopped I forced myself to start coughing, and when that didn't work, I shoved two of my fingers into the back of my throat until all that came out was yellowish-clear like orange juice. I wiped the tears from my eyes and drank some water that went down sweet out of the sink, then I went to work.

I'D STARTED CALLING MY PARENTS, but only when I knew that they wouldn't be home. Since I'd been working there I'd been collecting the coins and lighters and the pocket things people dropped from the roller coasters that snaked above Camp Snoopy's main floor. On my break I took some of the quarters to the phone bank and dialed up my old house. I hadn't thought much about the Oxy since I quit Lawson, but as I finished thumbing the coins into the slot and they'd clattered through the payphone's guts, metal and hollow, it was like an alarm went off in my blood. There was a click and the phone started ringing, soft and far away, underwater. I wanted to be that way. Still here but somehow separate, treated and ready to sleep or work, thinking slow or not at all like I was back in my bedroom, just me and my friend the ceiling.

The receiver was damp from my breath and pressed too close to my cheek, hugging my jawline. The wait got worse at the end of each ring. I just wanted to get to the answering machine. I just wanted to hear my mom say, "Hi, you've reached the Rudens—Janet, Mark, and Mike. Please leave your name, number, and a message after the tone, and we'll get back to you just as soon as we can." It wouldn't be much, but it would be enough. Just for today.

Finally the message played through, and I hung up just before the tone, then pressed the coin return. As soon as my change fell into the tray, I was thumbing it back into the payphone. I knew both my parents would be at work, but somehow hearing the months-old ghost of my mom's voice on the machine confirmed it. Janet and Mark aren't in right now, but they'll get back to you soon. This time the faraway ringing was duller, comfortable. I paid attention to my mom's breathing on the message machine. The way her voice picked up and hit the syllables clean and smooth when she said "Mark and Mike"—her two favorite things. This time I stayed on the line a heartbeat after the tone, long enough to hear myself breathing through the receiver. The breath she would hear on the recording when she came home and wonder if it was me. I put the phone back in its cradle and hit the coin return again, but the call had connected and the proof of life I'd left for later cost fifty cents.

The phone rang. It was the kind of thing you never expect, the kind of thing you forget about. That even a payphone has a number, that it can ring anytime, and if anybody is there they'll hear it and feel like they have to pick it up because the phone is ringing and goddamn it, isn't somebody going to answer that? It happened before I could really think about it, but I stopped myself short of saying hello. I just breathed.

"Mike? Honey, is that you?" Mom asked. Her voice was different than it was on the recording. More cracked around the edges. Used to crying and shouting, more careful than hopeful. "Mike, sweetie, where are you? It's okay, we just want you to come home. We're sorry." I breathed shallow into the mouthpiece. "We love you, we miss you. Please, just say something." I hung up, quick and violent, like I'd picked up a hot pan. The breath came syncopated and shaky now. I wanted to stop moving.

The sweat came back, even faster than before. I thought about Andy, busted open on the floor of Camp Snoopy the way my parents had probably been imagining me, in a ditch somewhere with too much blood and bone on the outside, never coming home. Her hand hit my shoulder warm and soft but I still jumped.

"Mikey, you all right?" Maggie asked. She looked tired, raccoon-eyed with her skin tight across her cheekbones, hair pulling against her forehead like it was the only thing keeping her eyes open. She was still touching me.

I felt like my face was twitching, reaching a rolling boil on the surface and she could see everything. "Yeah, yeah. I'm okay," I said, but I couldn't even convince myself.

"Who was on the phone?" she asked, taking her hand off my shoulder and it was one less thing to deal with. Just enough to level me out, if only for a minute.

"Oh, just some pervert, it was really weird—" I was cut off by the phone ringing, urgent and monotonous, a tornado siren.

Maggie snatched the phone up. "Hey, listen, creep. Fuck off with this shit or I'm calling the cops," she said, and slammed the receiver back into its cradle. She turned to me and exhaled sharp. "Look, Mikey, I wanted to talk to you about what happened yesterday. You didn't look good in the meeting this morning. I don't feel good about all this corporate shit either. I wanted you to know that I'm feeling fucked up about it too. I mean, that Andy kid. Jesus. If you wanted to like . . . talk about it or something, we can." She'd gotten closer to me when she answered the phone, and now we were both partway into the cubby, our body heat touching.

I wanted to tell her everything. I wanted to tell her that I was a fuck-up who took so many pills his parents sent him to Minnesota just to get him to stop. That I'd accidentally hitched a ride here because I was half in love with Carly, the girl next door, but now she'd be here soon with her family and maybe my parents if they looked up the number from this payphone and now all these things from far away were coming toward us to ruin everything. That she'd just met my mom. That when Andy Pfeiffer hit the ground it had made a sound like ripping out a baby tooth. The kind of sound that comes from inside your head, that you can't tell if you're hearing it or feeling it but it's somehow both and it smells like blood. The sound I can't stop hearing. That I just want to sit on a couch with Maggie in a basement and watch movies but really be watching her, breathing slower and slower until she's asleep on my shoulder like the best kind of hug, full of trust and warmth and forever because dreams are timeless.

"I gotta go," was what I came up with.

Maggie looked at me soft, like she understood that I couldn't let any of it out. Not today. "All right, Mikey. Well, keep your shit together. And let me know if you want to talk later. It's all right, you know. This isn't easy," she said.

"Yeah," I said. "It's not."   ▯

► I'D STARTED CALLING MY PARENTS, BUT ONLY WHEN I KNEW THEY WOULDN'T BE HOME.

angela sloan

ANGELA SLOAN received her Bachelor's as well as Master's Degrees in English Literature and Creative Writing from Longwood University in 2010 and 2012, respectively. She grew up on a farm in Virginia and has an identical twin sister; she lives and works in New York City. This is her second publication by Three Rooms Press.

THE LOVESICK PICTURE SHOW

1.

FLORA IS SPENDING THE RAINY Tuesday afternoon of her twenty-fifth birthday alone in Manhattan in a darkened movie house. She decides to see the schmaltzy romantic comedy instead of the gory slasher flick. She buys a large box of popcorn and eats it all, licking her fingers after each piece, between sips of a large Coke.

2.

SHE MET JACK TWO MONTHS earlier on an equally rainy afternoon at a dry cleaners near the Village. He was wearing a tweed jacket. She wore a blue silk blouse and a black knee-length skirt. They decided to go into a café next door: he had a cup of black coffee and she had a slice of strawberry pie with whipped cream and chocolate shavings. He complimented her pink lipstick and long black hair; he told her she looked like Snow White. They decided—before her pie and

his coffee were quite finished—to go back to her apartment
and have sex.

3.

THEIR SECOND DATE, THEY CONCLUDED, should be something
fun and frivolous, something neither of them had ever done
before. They decided to visit a porno theater: one of the only
ones left in the city. They shared an Uber all the way to
Brooklyn. The woman in the vintage movie was Seka: she
had a Marilyn Monroe-type hairdo, beautiful, large natural
breasts, a small heart tattoo on her left thigh, and glossy red
lips. She wore strappy gold high heels while having sex with a
man with black chest hair. Flora didn't like the movie very
much, but Jack was transfixed, even when Flora leaned over
to give him oral sex. They left the theater and stopped at a
corner hotdog stand: he had a frankfurter with sauerkraut
and mustard, but she didn't want anything.

4.

FLORA CALLED HER BEST FRIEND—A kindergarten school
teacher named Christine—the next week. They decided to go
to the Quentin Tarantino double-feature at the IFC Center:
they saw *Reservoir Dogs* and *Pulp Fiction*. They ate Milk Duds
and Red Hots and held hands. Afterward, they walked around
the neighborhood and smoked menthol cigarettes.

"I'm seeing a new guy: his name is Jack. He teaches Film
Studies at Columbia. I think he's married or something. All
we do is have sex. I don't even think he likes real movies,
only the dirty ones," Flora said.

"At least you have a date—all I do is wash my hair and go to the dog park."

"There's nothing wrong with that, Chris."

"Harold got the dog when we split up," she said. She tossed her cigarette into the gutter and lit another.

5.

FLORA WENT TO THE CINEMA every day that week. She saw the same movie each day, and wore the same dress.

6.

SHE CALLED JACK AT HIS office fifteen times that Wednesday evening. She left a message on his answering machine telling him that she missed him, and that she was starting to fall in love. She told him that she had worn the same dress, with the small stain from his semen, ever since they went to the porno theater a week earlier.

7.

JACK DIDN'T RETURN HER CALL, so she decided to look up his home telephone number in the white pages and call him. A woman with an English accent answered and she could hear piano music and ice clinking in glass tumblers and laughter and many voices in the background. One of the voices belonged to Jack. She could hear him asking the woman who was calling. Flora pretended to have dialed the wrong number and hung up.

8.

JACK SHOWED UP AT HER apartment the next week. He asked for a drink. They had vermouth cassis and talked about their sexual fantasies. Jack said that he wanted to be tied up with a curly telephone cord, while all Flora could say was that she wanted to get married and have a child. *A Place in the Sun* was playing on Turner Classic Movies on the television. She could smell his wife's gardenia perfume.

9.

THAT NIGHT, FLORA DREAMED THAT she was Dorothy in *The Wizard of Oz*. She was wearing the blue-and-white gingham dress and had braids and was carrying a brown basket. Toto was dead on the side of a winding road and Dorothy's feet were not wearing their pair of ruby-encrusted slippers, but were covered with blood.

10.

FLORA DRESSED IN FISHNET STOCKINGS and a black polyester merry widow. She frizzed her hair and painted on a pound of Max Factor: she was going to see *The Rocky Horror Picture Show*'s midnight showing at a revival movie house in Chelsea with Christine, who was going as Riff Raff.

11.

FLORA—WITH SMEARED LIPSTICK FROM kissing strangers during the musical number "Touch-a, Touch-a, Touch Me" and popcorn stuck in her aerosol-coated hairdo—spotted

Jack and his wife as they were leaving the theater. He did not see her, but she saw him with his arm around the nipped-waist sophisticate with whom he shared his bed and his heart. She asked Christine if she had any marijuana and if they could go back to her place and smoke it. She said no, but told her that she had a bottle of bourbon and they could take a hot bath together and watch reruns of *The Golden Girls* on television.

12.

FLORA CONTINUED TO SEE JACK around her neighborhood drycleaners where they first met. She sometimes saw him picking up silk dresses, and even once a fur coat. They didn't speak when they saw each other, but she remembered the gleam in his eyes when he spoke of being tied up, and the growl he tried to suppress in the back of his throat when he came in the porno theater. She decided to buy a pair of strappy gold high heels—just like the ones the actress in the adult movie had worn.

13.

NOW, SITTING IN THE THEATER on this day, her birthday, she slips her hand inside her trouser front, and touches herself slowly, thinking of Jack, while staring at the dark-haired man across the aisle. ❑

xingyue sarah he

XINGYUE SARAH HE is currently a student at the University of North Carolina at Chapel Hill. She studies English and creative writing, both in prose and script form. She enjoys writing about disabilities and illnesses and also hopes to bring a new voice into the canon of Asian–American literature. She has previously published a short story in UNC Chapel Hill's literary magazine *Cellar Door* and hopes to publish many more works to come.

MINNOWS

There was little wind that day, but they had raised the mast anyway. The little white boat floated on the sun-lit sea like a duck in a bathtub, bobbing with little purpose. The two lovers were hiding below deck, in their cramped cabin, sick of the sun, barely in their underwear.

He was writing the date with a Sharpie on the used condom. She watched him as she played with a loose thread on the bedcover.

"What are you doing?" she said.

"Chronicling," he said.

"Why?"

"You know, like Robinson Crusoe. Counting the days."

"Counting the days until I die?"

"Come on, that's not what I said."

She sat on the toilet without closing the door. He didn't look up but listened to the sound of her urine trickling down the tube, echoing through the cabin.

"You're not going to die," he said. "At least not because of that. Not while I'm around."

"That's convincing," she said, getting up from the toilet.

"I told you I'd take you on a little adventure, didn't I? And we're here, aren't we?"

"Well, we're not shipwrecked yet, so I guess you're doing pretty well," she said with a laugh.

He looked up from his writing. "Can you get me another Sharpie? This one isn't writing so well."

She walked around the small cabin, her head bent a little to the side.

"I don't think we've got any others," she said. "We didn't really pack that well did we?"

The Sharpie's felt tip kept slipping off of the rubber surface, but he carved until he had the date written in faint lines. Then he picked up the box of condoms and shook it with a smile.

"We've got what we need."

"Thanks for doing this," she said. "Even though you're going to get into a shitload of trouble with your dad."

"Of course," he said, looking out the cabin window through the metal, plastic, and glass to the quivering sea. "I'd do anything for you." He smiled at her like a five-year-old.

"I'll hold you to that," she said.

He looked out the cabin and saw the sea as a tranquil monster that could, at any moment, rebel against their rebellion and force them back to reality. He stared at it, daring it to rise. He would conquer it for her.

▯

SHE STOOD BY THE RAILING, her long velvet hair trailing behind her head like a flag. He chewed on some fishing wire with a rod in one hand and a dead minnow in the other. The sun set into the water like it was drowning, and the wind picked up.

"Are you going to take that job?" she said.

"I don't want to talk about that," he said. "Not here. Not with you."

"Why? You're going to need a job when you get back."

"You sound like my dad." He pierced the minnow's flesh.

"I didn't mean to—"

"Like when he told me I couldn't 'just run off to Europe with a useless art degree and spray-paint walls of old buildings.'" He cast his line out to sea. "That it wasn't 'the way to live.' That I needed a 'real job, real money,' to live."

He drew in the line without even waiting. The minnow was already half gone, its body broken at the spine.

"I'm sorry," she said.

She leaned over the rail, trying to feel the water with her fingers. He was afraid she would fall over, and he grabbed her by the waist.

"Aw, no, *I'm* sorry," he said.

"Let's just catch some fish."

They readjusted the weights, tried different hooks, pierced more minnows and cast their lines until the sun was long submerged under the water, a sea burial. They caught nothing. But the little pieces of minnow that always came back snug on the hook—a head with the eyeballs missing, or a tail and abdomen without its entrails—gave them goose bumps on the back of their necks and arms.

They ditched the rods on the deck and climbed into bed and ate sardines from a can and cold, buttered bread. They fell asleep in each other's arms among the empty cans and breadcrumbs, heart and bellies full.

HE WOKE UP TO THE sounds of the wind against the metal, the plastic, and glass. She was sleeping, but he nudged her with his knee anyway. He wanted to make sure he wasn't dreaming and that she was still there.

"Hey, do you hear that?" he asked.

"What?"

He watched her sit up, her hair trailing behind.

"It sounds really nasty out there," he said.

"Do you think we'll be okay?" she said as she rubbed her eyes.

He didn't answer but wrapped his arms around her shoulders. They sat there in bed in silence, listening to the howling wind push against the boat until he could feel her snores where her head pressed against his chest. He laid her down and tugged the covers over her before sinking back into the bed.

He felt the ends of her hair tickle his cheek and figured a storm was coming. But if their boat were to tip over, he would be okay with it as long as the world turned upside down with them and he woke to find himself already in the afterlife, with her, no longer fearing death.

THE SUN WAS ALREADY UP when she shook him awake. She was standing ankle deep in sea water, her hands on her hips.

"I don't know if I like the idea of you quantifying the last of my days," she said.

"What happened?" he said, looking around.

"There was a storm last night," she said. "We might be drowning."

"What?"

He got up and went straight to the dashboard. He pushed some buttons and flipped some levers, growing more and more frustrated. She walked around splashing the water as if she were a ten-year-old with new rain boots.

"Our power is shot. We aren't going to be able to start the motor."

She shrugged. "We've been anchored anyways."

For a moment, he forgot about the leaking ship and just stared at her.

"What? We're not planning on going anywhere," she said with a smile. "It's not like we're *dying*."

He tried to smile back but couldn't, so he made his way to the back of the living quarters, where he found the broken hose to the water heater and seawater seeping into the boat at a steady pace.

"Did you hear what I said earlier?" she asked, breaking the silence.

"Mmm?"

"I don't like the idea of you quantifying my days."

"No, of course not."

"You're not listening."

"Can you grab me some duct tape?" he said. "I'm going to see if I can stop this leak."

The water made his voice echo two pitches higher. The sound scared him. She splashed her way over to him, duct tape in hand.

"I wonder what it's like to have webbed feet," she said as he taped the broken hose. "Or a tail. To be able to live in the water, without having to be contained in this . . . this metal box."

"Like a mermaid?" he asked.

"Yeah. Like a mermaid."

"You wanted to be a poet right? You should write that down," he said and finished wrapping the hose. "All fixed up. I guess we're not drowning anymore."

They walked back to the cabin, and he got out a water pump.

"To be one with the shimmering expanse, to be at peace, to be infinite," she said. "How about that?"

"Sounds great."

They pumped the water out of the cabin in silence.

□

THE WATER WAS MOSTLY GONE, but some pooled in little dips and crevices around the cabin. The floors were slick, licked by the sea. He tried to start the engine again, but it sputtered, so he went to air out the wet inside the cabin.

He was peeling through the pages of the owner's manual, heavy with water, when he looked up and saw that she was on the deck trying to fish by herself, getting her hair tangled in the lines. Obscured by the sheet of glass, she looked like a specimen in a jar. Something to marvel at, to try to preserve, but something that had already long left this world.

He flipped through the soggy pages with just his thumb and forefinger, careful not to tear them. It took him a whole five minutes just to locate the emergency section and find page 387. *How to make an S.O.S. . . .* He read the whole section, just in case. Though the water hose had only been a minor setback—marring the romantic notions he'd had for the trip—the dead engine was the real issue. They'd be stuck here until he called the Coast Guard. But at that moment, anything was better than becoming an errand boy to some manager, a shrimp at a shrimp-packing factory.

"You look pissed."

She stood by the doorway, a piece of minnow on her cheek. "You look lovely," he said.

He motioned to his cheek where the fish was on hers, and she smudged it off with the back of her hand. She came around to his side and glanced at the opened manual.

"I wasn't going to, you know," he said, "make the S.O.S. At least not yet."

"That's fine."

"Wait." He got up and put the manual aside. "You're not worried?"

"No."

"You don't want to go back? Not even with the cabin flooding?"

"Nope," she said and began braiding her salt-sprayed hair. "I thought I would, by now, with the water hose breaking and all. That I'd feel claustrophobic or lost or something."

"But?"

"But the water hose broke, the sea came in. I mean, who knows what's going to happen next?" She pointed to the space heater, unplugged but damaged. "What if that breaks and sets our bed sheets on fire? What if the roof collapses? What if a shark comes and eats us?"

He could only look at her with a blank stare.

"I mean, what's the difference between that and getting holes drilled into my head? Or losing all my hair? Or being on fifty different pills in addition to having chemo pumped into me? Is it better to be so close to death and then live, or be alive only so you can die slower?"

"The first one?" He knew he answered wrong.

"No," she said, lowering her voice. "No. Nothing is better, because it's the same everywhere. Back home, on this boat, and anywhere else I could possibly try to escape to."

She sighed, left the cabin, and went to the farthest point out on the deck, away from him. He felt as if he was a student and she his teacher. A teacher who knew all the answers but only asked questions that made the answers more obscure. He sat in the cabin and listened to their battery-powered radio, scared to approach her. Scared of her.

BY THE MORNING, SHE SEEMED to have forgotten about her outburst and was sunnier than the sun. They tore the corners of four shrimp-flavored ramen packs and poured the flavoring into the bag of uncooked noodles. They shook and crushed the ramen and ate it like Cheetos, licking their fingers after.

"You know, we should probably stop eating so much sea-food-related stuff," she said sucking on her pinky.

"Why?" He looked in the fridge to see if he could find some beer.

"Well, if I'm going to be a mermaid and all."

"I guess so. Maybe we should just eat sea kelp or some-thing . . ." He found a single can of beer, behind an empty, crusty Ziploc bag. "Hey, you want to share this?"

He turned around only to find her on the cabin floor. She was shaking and her arms and legs were flopping on the floor like a fish, her hair spread out around her. She looked like an oracle, the moment before a message from the gods.

He dropped the beer and ran to her. He got on his hands and knees and wanted to help her but was afraid to touch her. He looked at the owner's manual, dry now, but wrin-kled. Nothing there on how to deal with seizures. He tried to remember, but all he could think of was how his scream might sound if he screamed, and how it would bounce off the walls of the cabin and come hurtling back at him.

Put something in her mouth was the best he could come up with, all he could remember. By the time he turned back to her she had stopped shaking but was on her back, gargling on her own spit. He turned her to her side and the spit came trickling out. It pooled on the floor, glistening.

"Hey," he said. "Are you okay?"

She nodded once.

"Do you want to get up?"

She shook her head.

"Do you need me to do anything?"

She shook her head again. He tried to approach her to comfort her, but when he looked at her limp body he felt a sudden wave of nausea hit the bottom of his stomach.

"Okay," he said and took a few steps back. "I'm just going to be over here. Just let me know if you do want something."

She made a murmuring sound. He opened the owner's manual, back to page 387. The pages crinkled like dried seaweed. He half read, half breathed, half listened.

▯

THEY SAT SHOULDER TO SHOULDER with the bed sheet wrapped around them. They felt cold inside the cabin, despite the sun. He didn't want to use the space heater—her words from earlier still lingering in his head. He didn't want to burn, now that they only had a couple of hours before the Coast Guard would come.

"I'm sorry that I couldn't help," he said.

"It's fine," she said. "I wouldn't expect you to."

"Well I probably should have studied the symptoms or something beforehand."

"There's no manual for this kind of thing." She wiggled out of their bed sheet cocoon. She walked up to the deck, and without turning her head, said, "I don't want them to come."

"What?" he asked, unable to hear her, her voice drowned out by the walls separating them and the sea pushing against their boat.

"I said I don't want the Coast Guard to come. I don't want to go back."

He came to the deck and stood on the opposite side. He tried to look at her, but the sun was in his eyes and the wind blew her hair over her face.

"You have to."

"Why do I have to?"

"Because you have to get treatment. You have to get better."

She turned away from him and bent over the side. She reached with one hand to the water, the other grasping the rails.

"I'm not going to get better," she said. "I just want to always be here. In this place. Right here, right now."

They didn't speak for a minute. She took the pail of minnows, fishing bait now long dead, and handfed the hungry waters each little fish, sliding them in gently between waves. He just watched her as she moved: her long hair blowing, sunburned shoulders, strong arms, the skin on her legs chapped from too much salt air and reflecting the sun like little broken mirrors, like iridescent scales.

"Let's share that beer I found." He had to say something.

He wanted to go to the cabin, to be encased by the metal, plastic, and glass and not vulnerable out in the open. He took his time looking for the beer, even though he knew it was lying by the bed, underneath the crumpled bed sheet that had only just held them together. The cabin floor was glossy, wet. He went to the water heater and found the duct tape hadn't sealed properly, and water was leaking back into the cabin. He didn't bother re-taping the hose.

He decided he took enough time, reached under the bed sheet on the floor, which was soaking up the sea, and grabbed the beer can. Stuck at the bottom of the can was the used condom with a faint date etched across. He tried to shake it off. When he couldn't, he walked it up to the deck to show her, to maybe make her laugh.

Just as he stepped on deck, he saw a flash of hair and two iridescent-scaled legs, pressed together as one, extended long, pointed to the sky. Then gone. Then a splash in the water. He ran over to where she had been and looked over the rails.

"Melinda!" He said her name as loud as he could.

She would surface soon, hair thick and wet around her shoulders with that joking smile on her face. She would laugh at him for being so silly and ask him to join her in the water, one last swim before heading back. She would agree to go back and let the doctors treat her, save her. She would, she would. She had to.

He called her name one more time. The sea swallowed his voice. The waters below bubbled a little and then became soft, smooth waves. He dropped the can he was holding into the water. The can sank but the condom floated, in its transparency it became like the sea until it was nothing but a faint date written in Sharpie. The minnows floated in a circle around it, their pellucid bodies animated in dance. Then as the waters calmed, they fell away one by one, reclaimed by the sea. ❑

joshua tuttle

JOSHUA TUTTLE is a US Army Veteran, Eagle Scout, and Dungeon Master, and in a former life he was an IT engineer. He studies Computer Science and English at Whitworth University in Spokane, Washington. He has been published in *Script* and an RPG supplement entitled "The Demonic Interference at New Ritupis Church" was recently published on *DriveThruRPG*. Schedules permitting, his Gothic Horror D&D game meets weekly on Sundays. In his remaining spare time, Josh runs the Spooky Scary Skeletons Literary and Horror Society, which meets twice monthly in Spokane, Washington. Public-facing meeting notes can be found at www.spookyscarysociety.com.

ON CALL

never sleep well when I'm on call. I'm a junior engineer at an engineering and IT support firm, and our biggest client is a large medical device company. We're responsible for keeping their servers running, and they need to keep running twenty-four seven. So, every six weeks, it's my turn to go on call and respond to issues as they arise. Most of the time things are pretty quiet, but unfortunately I'll get a page any time an email is sent to a particular email address. I say unfortunate because this email address has managed to end up on a few spam lists over the years, and very few things make me more angry than to be woken up in the middle of the night so that I can close a ticket that reads: "Let us tell you about how amazing HP's new customer support portal is!"

So no, I don't sleep well while I'm on call. I used to, and for a long time no one realized. One day I missed an important ticket because I had set my phone to silent. After a very public thrashing by my boss, I resolved never to do this again. Now, I sleep lightly, like I learned in the Army, so that

I can respond to anything that goes wrong. This morning was no different.

When I got out of the Army three years ago, the options were pay half my income in rent or live with my father and help put my sister through college. It was an easy choice, though not without drawbacks. I like to wake up around nine fifteen and be in the office by about ten. My father gets up earlier than me, as he tries to be at his desk by nine. This means that my last couple of hours of sleep are not as restful, even though I nailed a blanket over my window to keep out the morning sunlight. When he is not singing in the shower (which gets piped right into my room through the air ducts, even though I have mine closed), he's bumbling around in the kitchen getting his coffee and breakfast ready.

I got woken up by a page from my cell phone about half an hour ago. I checked the message and groaned after I logged into the ticketing system (a pain in the butt to do from my phone, by the way) once I discovered it was merely an "FYI." I briefly checked my email, and saw that I had new visitors on Zoosk. I wasn't optimistic; I don't have a picture up yet, so they are probably just bots. I'll check the photos out later today and see if they are any good. It's now eight fifteen in the morning. I've heard my father in the living room and kitchen since I woke up. He's been making a lot of noise, and it sounds like a lot of thumping, like he is opening and closing every cabinet and drawer we have and shuffling things around.

I should go back to sleep, but I can't. It isn't even the noise my father is making, per se. It's the fact that my father shouldn't be making *any* noise. After a particularly rough day yesterday I finally snapped and made sure of that. I took one of the new steak knives my sister and I got him for Christmas and sliced open his throat so I could sleep in peace, spam tickets willing. I checked on him a moment ago when I got up to get my laptop. He was still in his room, lying in a drying pool of his own room-temperature blood. But I still hear noises in the kitchen. I don't want to leave my room again. I've got my laptop charger in here with me.

Maybe I'll work from home today. ⬛

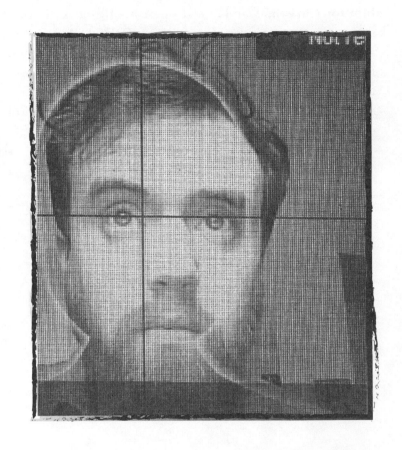

tyler barton

TYLER BARTON is a teacher and workshop leader from southcentral Pennsylvania. He is the fiction editor of *Third Point Press* and an MFA candidate at Minnesota State University. His stories have appeared in *Matter Press, Whiskey Paper, Knee-Jerk Magazine,* and elsewhere. Links to many of these stories can be found at tsbarton.com. Follow him @goftyler.

TEN THINGS
I LEARNED
SINCE COLLEGE

There's a Goodwill right on the close edge of York, PA. It probably ain't even part of the shopping district, technically. (#1: That "ain't" is still a word).

Kinda like how York is the nation's very first capital, this Goodwill is the very first store.

That's reason one my mom agrees to drive us out there; it's close, easy on gas. Second is, "Us girls do need clothes." February is over but the snow's still hanging on, and my boots don't keep out wet when I'm shoveling the walk for the ten-spot our landlord'll give me.

Most importantly, this Goodwill has an attachment on the side called the Bargain Room. It's like a bonus store, owned and operated by the same company, but its squatter and without color, a Better Will for those poorer folk. Those folk like Mom and me fit in there at the Bargain Room.

Since I left MSU we shop here. Before college we actually went to the mall and bought new clothes every time the season turned. Then during college, it was mostly just Target, but

Mom wouldn't stoop to Walmart. Things changed though, since my college days ended.

We skipped right over Walmart on the ladder down.

And we started shopping at this Goodwill, after Mom had spent all her money on my school for five and a half years, after three or four major changes, after I lost the scholarship with the DUI, and the FAFSA grants with the academic probation, after I made us regular paupers coming home with a 2.1 GPA to live jobless with her for this whole past year, after the poorly attended graduation party and empty congrats cards. (#2: That folks don't like to give to you if you got everything given to you anyways, especially not if you don't seem to make very hard an effort to get home for Thanksgivings, birthdays, even funerals.)

But finally, since the time Mom's boss at the plant broke the news of the efficiency agency's findings and her job's new nonexistence, we switched to shopping at only the Bargain Room part of the building.

On the drive over Mom likes to take her "shortcut." (#3: That there are no shortcuts.) This takes us the roundabout way to town so she can drive slow through old Heritage Heights where all the biggest yards and grandest mansions in the county are.

This one house, for example, has a fountain bigger than our apartment.

This other has a crazybig 3-D wood carving of a moose in the front garden, and I bet they ain't ever seen a real moose besides maybe some stuffed heads hanging in their parlor rooms.

I see now, driving through, that these properties are *expansive*—all that space looking unused and pointless. I think it's mainly so you know how *expensive* the places are. (#4: That the point of getting rich is to have your house as far away from other houses as possible, and #5: that the poorer you are, the more crammed together you are, as people.)

I certainly sense this in the Bargain Room, where there's not so much racks and shelves of clothing as there is just troughs. When we get there we're one of the many families set out to dig through these big wooden cases full of unsorted, unfolded clothing.

The whole room is really just two sections: clothes and shoes. I go to the shoes section, where there ain't even pairs, just single shoes of all sizes thrown in together in this open box. It reminds me of a ball pit at the mall arcade, and I just want to dive in. But I can't because I'm squeezed in there with about eight other people, pawing through, looking for a pair that fit or match.

It's more like a barn, I suppose, than a room, with these long messy trays. Sometimes I call it the Bargain Barn, which obviously fits and has a better ring to it. Not that I'm being mean, just that with the place so plain and all the structures made of wood and nails it really feels like we're all coming to feed there like cattle.

In there at the Bargain Room there's more women like Mom and me. In college, a lot of girls were cutting their hair off short, but the women here let it grow long and don't keep it well. It sticks out places and defies gravity. It works its way out of buns and musses up ties and clips and bobby pins. One woman near me has a tuft somehow going straight up like Marge Simpson except it ain't blue. (#6: That people like to say something with their hair, or else they say nothing at all, which is kind of a way of communicating something anyhow.)

A whole group of girls come in wearing white shoes with white pants and dirty, once-white T-shirts. Don't we know laundry is expensive.

There's also the woman who pushes her son in a stroller though he's nearly nine, or looks it. Somehow it's allowed that people bring dogs in too, and they do. Under the trough I'm at this little terrier's tearing up a clog.

Like I said Mom stays over at the clothes trough. She searches for dresses that fit me or at least have all the necessary buttons, a zipper that works. She's says she's not, but she's always looking for my new interview clothes.

As if that'll ever happen.

I've been down to the temp agency a few times now and jack's happened as a result. In fact, this last time the lady actually told me to go home and draw up this list. She said, "Catalogue what you feel you've learned from your college experience." She thinks this can help me pick what $7.25/hr job I'd like best. (#6: That General Studies might not be the most practical thing to get a degree in.)

Still I shouldn't bitch.

At least I got to go to school, and we ain't bankrupt yet. At least we got the paper says I'm a bachelor of art, got it hanging there above the couch beside the picture of my grandma, the only one who liked my decision to enroll out in Michigan anyhow, the one who died as I was starting my junior year, whose funeral I didn't make it home for. Anyway, the paper is at least something, I think.

And plus, this girl I know who graduated Summa Cum Laude still don't got a job either because I keep up with her on Facebook. (#7: That grades still don't mean shit no matter who's pretending or how hard.)

No, I know I got it made better than a lot of folk, so I don't normally bitch. And I really ain't. It's just I'm thinking about this list as I dig through the shoe trough looking for a match to this snow boot I found might fit. I'm thinking the one thing I actually did learn in college had to do with that broken record the lib arts classes kept playing us: this Empathy, Empathy. (#8: That empathy can be condescending as any human emotion. Empathy: all of educated America standing elbow to elbow in this great expansive field with each one feeling and experiencing but really only pretending to experience or feel everything anyone's ever felt or thought or gone through, a big shiny tear coming down off their right eyes.)

No, I ain't down here teary-eyed among folk at the shoe trough, *emp*athizing. I don't feel nothing but closeness. I don't pretend to know a thing about how they all feel or what it is they seen.

I just put my head down and dig, smiling that I still got the chance to. (#9: That if those shiny tears are starting to stream their way down my mom's face, or if she's choking back a big cry, as the man at the counter hands her back her card with that fake frown and head-shaking apology act, I sure as hell don't see nothing.)

On the drive home Mom gives me hell about not looking for interview clothes, even though I promise that I did. She deals with rejection like I do, by getting pissed. This is why I dropped my expectations, why talking to the temp lady feels like an ass-pain chore, why my grades were so whatever.

"I just want you to look. You might find something," she says to the windshield.

She don't believe that I tried and keeps on lecturing with her face still wet from where she cried. Just driving and not quite crying and simply wringing me out. Her spiel reminds me of my professors. Potential, measurements, competition. Everything I know about America. I make the face that says I'm not listening, but it ain't possible not to hear what she's saying.

By the time we reach our road, while she struggles like hell to park parallel, I admit to some old impulse shaking loose, like when you're shoveling and you find something buried under layers of snow. As she opens her door, I promise myself next time I will really try. I'll look harder. I clench my old jeans in my right fist, grab the handle with my left, and climb out. (#10: That hope just boils like anger.)   ⬛

▶ **I JUST PUT MY HEAD DOWN AND DIG, SMILING THAT I STILL GOT THE CHANCE TO.**

aaron thorpe

Aaron Thorpe is a New York native living in Georgia. He is an alumni of Borough of Manhattan Community College, where he also worked as an English tutor for two years. In 2013 he received the W. W. Norton Award for Excellence in Fiction. As of this writing, he is a grassroots organizer for Bernie 2016. For more of his work, visit his blog at cockroachesandbutterflies.wordpress.com.

ON LOVING LIKE A HUMAN

PART 1, VIA TWENTY-FIRST-CENTURY NARRATIVE
SCENARIO-TYPE THOUGHT EXPERIMENTS—
FOR POSTHUMANS, EXTRATERRESTRIAL ANTHROPOLOGISTS,
AND HIGHLY EVOLVED/SELF-AWARE DOLPHINS OR
CEPHALOPODS OF TERRESTRIAL ORIGIN—OR PERHAPS THE
AVERAGE TWENTY-FIRST-CENTURY HUMAN WHO HAS MANY
FOLLOWERS, "FRIENDS," AND REAL-LIFE ACQUAINTANCES
BUT NOT ONE MEANINGFUL RELATIONSHIP

Hey there. If you're reading this, human civilization as it was once known—the sprawling cities, art, language, religion, the Internet—is long gone. I'm sure Earth looks very different now. If two-way communication across the aging expanse were possible, I'd love to hear about it: dense woods where great cities once stood, oceans atop ancient deserts, etc. But although Earth may change, other seemingly less permanent things do not. The heart of the caveman and the heart of the average twenty-first-century human both beat to the same rhythm. Speaking of which, the human heart—drawn thusly (♥)—was a symbol of a deep-felt, ineffable, and often dualistic emotion: love.

I won't presume love does not exist in your time, among your species—be you posthuman, sentient squid, or otherwise. It may very well be the moral polestar around which your civilization orbits, with constitutions and holy books committed to love in practice and not in theory. In any case, love in my era was unique but somewhat absent and so wholly necessary, and on the off chance that it has been forgotten since then, Part 1 of this treatise will provide an introductory overview. The following scenarios are not meant to be interpreted as firsthand accounts, or even factual; rather, think of them as allegorical, symptomatic.

SCENARIO A:
SPOOKY ACTION AT A DISTANCE

JOHN AND MEI LIVE IN the same era but reside in different time zones. When his sun is setting, hers is rising. They meet the day before Mei is to return home, across an ocean and two continents. They are hopelessly, magnetically drawn to one another upon initial visibility, if you can believe it. Neither knows what hit them. They are doomed. (That was the thing about love in my time: it had no rationale and did not care where and when and between whom it bloomed, like some hardy plant.)

As her plane is readying for take-off, Mei texts John: *I want to make us possible.* John replies: *Me too.* Mei writes back: *But do you know what I mean? I do,* says John.

Fortunately, modern technology (text messaging, email, video chat, the rare phone call) makes interfacing between John and Mei possible despite the distance, only both are worried about coming across as awkward and dull and thus unlikeable. Twenty-first-century technology is great for remote communication but sorely inadequate at conveyance. John fears he may be seen as lazy and unmotivated because he's not in school or working and still lives with his folks. He feels that if he openly expresses himself, his frustration and his dreams, he will unduly burden Mei, a woman he's only just met but is quantumly entangled with. Mei is embarrassed by her poor English and does not want John to judge her, even though she knows he doesn't, won't. And so John and Mei cope with their respective insecurities by continuously referencing the day they met (*Happiest day of my life*, John writes; *Mine too*, Mei replies) and by building upon their self-perceived ideal selves that both feel like they projected into the other's mind that day, a personality so dynamic and arresting and not unlike-able. Otherwise the conversation drags on, albeit tactfully, like a match between two chess masters.

And this actually works, this projection and embellishment of their respective selves of a single day, creating a positive feedback loop in which John and Mei are increasingly attracted to persons who arguably do not exist. And as each becomes more and more comfortable with this person both helped to create, John and Mei discover these persons have many things in common and their worldviews run just about parallel. And then, undeterred by the seven-thousand-plus miles between them, John and Mei begin "cybering" (a twenty-first-century term for simulated coitus using communicative technology, usually involving clumsy yet surprisingly stimulating essay-length messages re: What I Would Do to You if You Were Here and reciprocal pixelated masturbation via webcam). All this inevitably leads to John and Mei falling in love with Projection Mei and Projection John, respectively. They begin dating and promise to meet again, somehow.

This is love: born of moments, memories, circumstance. Love texting him at four in his morning because she just got out of work and her setting sun reminds her of him. Love making him respond even though he wants to sleep. A love addictive, inexorable, and exhausting. Yet why do John and Mei, individually, sub rosa, catch themselves rationalizing its legitimacy?

[▯]

Scenario B:
The New

I'm sitting in the Starbucks at Union Square waiting for Zed, who's forever late. He's known since last week that I wanted to meet with him, or at least he should have if he checked his voicemail and inboxes. Reaching him has been harder than usual. But I'm sure he'll come. He'll rise from his computer desk for a bathroom break, half-starved and unshowered, eyes glassy with fatigue. As he's standing over the toilet he'll suddenly remember and slap his forehead in self-admonishment. He'll sprint out of the bathroom without flushing or zipping up his fly and pull on whatever clothes smell cleanest. In less than five minutes he'll be out of the apartment and running to the subway, but when he's halfway there he'll stop, riffle through his pockets, slap his forehead again, and run back to unplug the multiple devices he's left charging: the three or sometimes four cutting-edge smartphones he's currently testing, including the one he refers to as his "daily driver"; the wireless hi-fi headphones; the smartwatch. He'll debate whether to bring the Google Glass before abandoning the idea, recalling how much I fucking hate it when he wears that thing in public. Fully equipped and connected, he'll run back out and into the subway and onto the uptown 4 to 14th Street. He'll bumble into Starbucks and apologize to the two women exiting whose coffee he nearly sent aground. He'll apologize to me, too, before he even completely makes it over to where I sit by the window. I'll be like, *It's cool, don't worry, I've only been waiting an hour,* and it'll be totally sincere and not sarcastic at all. He'll keep saying sorry until he sees my right brow arch in mild annoyance and then ask if I want anything, to which I'll say, *No, I'm okay.* He'll order coffee and scones anyway because he hasn't eaten since breakfast. I'll sit and wait while he's at the counter, staring into the hollow my semi-clasped hands have made. And when he comes back, sets my unwanted coffee/scone in front of me, and sits down, he'll ask, *So, what's up?* and I'll tell him outright that I'm pregnant.

The fear in his eyes will be less intense than I expected, and I'll wonder if he sensed this was coming. That of the many consequences of two opposite-sex BFFs hooking up, this was the one to befall us. Maybe, like me, after the hookup, he couldn't sleep at night and in the morning fought the urge to remain in bed with the covers pulled over his head. Maybe he's as conflicted as I am and I'll see it on his face—no more guesswork from the tone of his texts, no more hoping and dreaming.

Then again, how can anything good come from this? Unlike me, Zed has a promising career as a consumer tech analyst; he lives on his own in his Brooklyn studio filled with the latest gadgets; he's made significant progress tackling his student debt and doesn't need anything else weighing him down. He has more followers on Twitter and Instagram than people I'll ever meet personally, a million-plus subscribers to his YouTube channel. He goes outside and people recognize him.

But this shouldn't be about him, or even me. It should be about us. About whatever is unfurling inside me.

He'll ask if I'm sure. I'll pull the strip in the small Ziploc bag out of my pocket and show him. I won't be discreet. He won't care. He'll study it like a litmus test indicating his fate. He'll sigh through his nose and hand it back. Then he'll do one of two things:

He'll propose that I get rid of it, trying to be as delicate as possible, the baritone in his voice softening to something less imposing. He'll offer to pay for the pill. A quick Google search with one of the phones will tell him how much it'll cost, how soon I can take it. Insurance might cover it, he'll say. I know all this already. One of my roommates at Purchase took the pill after her boyfriend knocked her up on a weekend visit, so I have a pretty good idea of what will happen if I take it, too. But I won't fight him; who am I to steal his future, to pull up the yellow brick road beneath his feet? He'll tell me he'll be there every step of the way. That I won't be alone. When it's all said and done, though, I'll go back to my life and he'll go back to his, and I'll convince myself that it was for the best.

Or:

He'll reach across the table and hold my hand. I'll think it's funny how something as simple as being touched that way can make you cry. He'll say it's up to me—whatever I want to do, he'll be there. This time I'll believe him. *If you want to keep it—is it right to call it an"it"?—that's okay, because.* . . . He won't have to say "I love you." I'll see it on his face. But I'll say it if he does, when he comes. Hell, I bet he's on his way right now.

◻

Scenario C:
Suppose

For argument's sake, let's suppose you—no—let's just say your friend is having a moral and existential crisis. The kind that challenges everything this friend has ever believed in and that forces them to do the insanely difficult work of scrutinizing this lifelong set of beliefs, as if it had never been introduced to your friend as a child by their own indoctrinated parents. To view these beliefs from a plateau of objectivity. This friend is like a sibling to you. You two grew up riding bikes together and playing Nintendo and, when you were older, chasing members of the opposite sex and trying beer and even a little weed. One of these beliefs—and though it's just a tiny part, millions of people who also subscribe to this set of beliefs think this part is crucial—denounces mingling with or being drawn to or falling in love with, whatever, a certain group of people. Those who believe this particular belief, especially your friend's parents, claim these people are amoral; not *im* moral, but *a* moral, meaning they don't know right from wrong because they haven't been blessed with the superlative belief from which all the other beliefs stem. Your friend's parents have pretty much spent all their parental energies preventing your friend from mingling with, being drawn to, loving, etc. these morally vapid people. As for you, this is yet another one of those crises you have to spin around by the shoulders and confront because you too have been brought up with this superlative belief and all the secondary beliefs—although now, as a somewhat-adult, you've shunned them. You still play Nintendo and chase members of the opposite sex and drink beer and smoke weed, but you do all this alone because you and your friend are no longer as close. Yet the superlative belief lingers, and sometimes you find yourself feeling so sickeningly guilty you want to drop to your knees and press your palms together and do something you haven't done in a long-ass time.

But this is beside the point. Even though you and this friend aren't as physically and emotionally close as you once were, your friend calls you one night when you're high, crying. Your friend says they've not only mingled with and become drawn to one of these amoral people, but they also love this person and then some. The one fucking thing they promised their parents, themselves, etc. that they would never do, they've gone and done it. They're ashamed and also terrified because, as crazy as it sounds, another belief in this set of beliefs millions subscribe to is that if you spend your whole life doing the right thing, you'll be rewarded when you die with eternal bliss. Your friend is scared for their soul. And, even worse, since your friend did what they did with who they did it with, this means your friend is one of the amoral. They still believe in the superlative, they say, which makes things more complicated: If they believe but are amoral, then did they ever really believe to begin with, as a child? Have they always been amoral? How is it possible to both believe and not to? The friend's contradictions penetrate your high. Your head starts to hurt. You can hear the snot bubbling in their nose as they sob. They're begging you to tell them what to do like you used to. So . . . what do you say? Your conviction is not what it used to be, with your overflowing wastebasket of beer cans and roach clips, your mind swarming with filth. If only you could step outside of yourself and embrace this other person, the superlative watching.

SCENARIO A-1:
SMEARED OUT IN EQUAL PARTS

THREE YEARS HAVE PASSED SINCE John and Mei's first/last vis-à-vis encounter. Much has changed: John is working a minimum-wage job and is in a committed relationship with a coworker, and Mei, upon winning the Green Card Lottery, is preparing to relocate to the States, in New York, where John lives. What has not changed is the memory of that single day three years ago, preserved by both in shimmering vividness. Despite the failed experiment of their intercontinental romance, they still interface via twenty-first-century tech, though their communication slowed once John began dating Abby; he deletes emails/text messages/call history/ etc., all evidence of his association with Mei. This makes him feel like shit, especially because Abby knows of Mei after the obligatory post-coitus We're-Getting-Pretty-Serious-So-We-Should-Discuss-Our-Romantic-History talk they had. But she has made the fatal mistake of placing too much trust in him, John knows, and she assumes he has ceased all communication with the woman she hesitates to call his ex.

Mei is also aware of John+Abby due to his own admission, but it doesn't feel real to her, and she doubts it feels legitimate to him, either. He often vents about how cold and dismissive Abby can be, citing the time on the subway when she accused a panhandler of being deceitful about his intentions "to use other people's hard-earned money to snort crack" and so on. Yet if Mei suggests that maybe John shouldn't be with someone so stony-hearted since he himself is such a sweet and thoughtful guy, he gets miffed and emphasizes his love for Abby. Mei says: *Okay*, and John goes: *Yeah*, and provides an excuse to end the conversation.

Still, when she tells him that she has won the lottery and plans to arrive in New York unnervingly soon for what he feels should be a process fraught with bureaucracy, his heart pounds in his throat. Each day afterward becomes more difficult for him to look Abby in the eye. He tries, but it's like staring into the sun. As they make nightly love at her place, John, who's always on top, buries his face in Abby's shoulder while he thrusts and thrusts and thrusts, eyes shut tight, the lucid imago of a smiling Mei pressing forward against the black.

I love Abby, he reminds himself every waking minute counting down to Mei's immigration. There is no doubt in his mind that he does. It's the kind of love that can be spread out before him like a map and traced from one point to the next. It has dates and locations and physical instances, a sort of love inconceivable with someone whose day ends as yours begins, John and Mei acknowledged. Whatever they had, if you could even call it love, was too dependent on the digital abstract—a binary affair of zeroes and ones. All the same, John is dreading Mei's impending arrival, so much so that when she asks if he can meet her at the airport to help take her things to where she'll be staying, he says he's not sure, he may have to work that evening.

Because if he sees her . . . then maybe he might find the courage to say the things he most wanted to say, the things he could not say through the phone but only in person. And although the things he would say would not be perfect, they would be true, and his eyes would warm as he said them— things that, till now, he could only express in her expanding absence. And she would be beautiful, more beautiful than he had remembered and not somewhere unseen and so imagined, her thoughts related to him by the shape of her sentences, not far-off and just a name, but presence with breath and voice and beauty. She would be happiness and frustration and wanting and kisses soft like whispers, a future he did not even know was possible. Did not even know was possible. Was possible. Possible.   ◻

tiffany ferentini

TIFFANY FERENTINI is a New York-based writer
and editor, and a graduate of Manhattanville
College's Master of Fine Arts in Creative Writing
program. Tiffany has served as an editor of the
Manhattanville Review, and is the current Marketing
Manager for Monkey Business International and
the Community Coordinator for AWP's LGBTQ
Caucus. Their short fiction and poetry have
appeared in the *Gambler* and *Off the Rocks,* the
LGBTQ Anthology of Newtown Writers Press.
They can be found on Twitter @ferenteeny.

GLITTER
AND GLUE

Well . . . you certainly don't look like a faggot."

This was the "hello" Ryan's Aunt Maybelle greeted him with as he stepped off the Greyhound bus, the sound of the parking lot gravel crunching beneath the weight of his worn-out Converse more welcoming than her husky voice, thick and heavy with the tar from her cherry-scented clove cigarettes. No "How are you feeling?"; no "How was the trip?" No, if she had welcomed him any other way, hailed him as anything other than her "faggot nephew," that's when he would have been discouraged.

Her voice sent his gaze downward, his eyes focusing on the ketchup stain on the tail of his button-down, the condiment having dyed the blue plaid purple. If he didn't look like a faggot, what *did* he look like? He certainly didn't look like himself, that was for sure. If he looked how he pleased, the wrinkles would be smoothed out of his shirt, the fabric crisp and the ketchup stain long removed. His underarms wouldn't be damp and rancid with the stench of three days' worth of sweat, and the smell of bus stop lavatories and gas stations would be washed out of his jeans.

Ryan wiped at the stained fabric of his button-down to no avail, the ketchup having long set in from a fallen French fry he couldn't remember purchasing or eating. Something gritty stuck to his hand and reflected in the afternoon sunlight, and only when he turned his palm upward did he realize it was glitter, the same glitter that had driven him out of his Houston house and onto a Wayne County-bound bus in the first place.

📱

FAIRY PRINCESS SHIT.

Fairy princess shit. That's what his pa said when he lugged Ryan's duffel bag out the door and to where he was standing on their lawn. Ryan had to duck to avoid getting beamed in the head; the bag landed half on the grass, half on the walkway, sounding as if whatever his pa had thrown in there died on impact. It made Ryan think for a moment his pa had packed up whatever useless knickknacks and pieces of junk he could find just so he could hear the satisfying crunch when the bag hit the ground—so he could know his son's few remaining pieces of clothing would be coated in needles of glass.

Ryan would get dressed and flecks of glass would settle under his armpits and prick his inner thighs, reminding him of the mess he had gotten himself into, and back home his father would smile.

"Got a call from the school you're suspended—and for what? Putting glitter in your sister's hair? Fairy princess shit!"

That morning Ryan'd convinced Lucille to let him do her hair and makeup before school. He needed practice for the school play that was coming up. *Macbeth.* He was in charge of the makeup and costumes. He still wasn't sure what he was going to do for the Three Witches, and he couldn't practice on himself, what with his wispy, cropped hair that his pa made him chop into a buzz cut. *I have one daughter already, I won't have you growing your hair out, too,* his pa had said. What he mostly hated was the long hours of helping his pa pick crops and tend to the fields; so much time in the sun would leave his scalp itchy and burned. He hated running a layer of suntan lotion through the fuzz on his head, even if it helped in the long run. Suntan lotion wasn't supposed to go in someone's hair. Fingers were.

Ryan had come up with the idea of using glitter for the Three Witches. Glitter around their eyes, glitter in their hair; he didn't give a shit if Shakespeare didn't have glitter back in his day—his sister looked beautiful: a beautiful, evocative witch who would haunt Macbeth's soul and change his life. When Macbeth would close his eyes at night, he'd still be able to see the witches' eyes in the black of his eyelids, the purple and gold outlining the almond slits, the flecks of color in their hair, like drops of blood, reminding Macbeth of his sin, haunting. Haunting.

Haunting.

He called it creative license. His school called it lice.

Ryan didn't even bother explaining to his pa that the school hadn't cared to consider that lice didn't sparkle. Didn't even bother explaining how they wouldn't listen when he told them it was a makeup test for the play. He didn't even bother explaining that they didn't even check Lucille for lice—just sent the two of them right on home, figuring if one farm kid had what looked like bugs crawling through her hair, her brother probably did too. Even if that brother barely had hair to crawl through.

He looked at Lucille through their living room window, her black eyes peering over the top of the couch, her hair hanging in thick, damp locks instead of its usual bouncy black curls. All the makeup had been washed from her face, the red wiped from her lips, the glitter vanquished from her hair. It'd probably clog the drain that night, giving his pa something else to growl about. *Growl* because Ryan wouldn't be there to yell at. Lucille just looked at him with her big, sad, farm-girl eyes that always made her look like she was about to cry, that always looked like they were saying the words that would never pass her lips: *I'm sorry.*

Of course she was sorry. She was always sorry; he knew she was. He didn't blame her for never standing up for him. She was younger than him, for one, and she took after their ma, for two.

His pa slammed the screen door on him, didn't even bother saying he didn't want him to come back because it went unspoken. Ryan threw over his shoulder the duffel bag he was grateful to have had thrown at his head.

With the leftover lunch money in his pocket he went to the bus stop pay phone and placed a long-distance call to his Aunt Maybelle in New York.

"Work?" She wheezed through the phone. "I don't know, boy. I know your type."

Ryan tried to ignore his pa's voice hissing in his ear: *Fairy princess shit.*

"My type?"

A pause. He heard her take a drag of her clove cigarette and exhale, and he swore he caught a whiff of the cherry tobacco through the phone line.

"Your type. All those hands of yours are good for is getting thread through needles and sticking your fingers in holes they don't belong."

His eyes went to his biceps bulging from the cotton of his plaid button-down, the result of those long hours working in the fields with his pa—and of pushing his body off the floor, out of stairwells or lockers, back when the bullies used to get him. His body grew strong not out of desire, but necessity. When he was younger Ryan longed for the day his voice would crack and his balls would drop, when his body matured and gave him the physical strength he needed to get by in the world. A caterpillar hardening into its cocoon, a young boy discovering his own chrysalis.

But before Ryan could revel in the feel of his muscles expanding and growing harder beneath his soft skin, before he could trace his fingertips across his newly defined arms and thighs and imagine what it would feel like if those fingers belonged to another man, the transformation had already been completed; the shell of his pupa long cracked. Suddenly he was taller and wider than the bullies and the five-by-one lockers they used to stuff him into, and had more strength and stamina than his pa. Ryan only realized when the bullies began to leave him alone at school, and when his pa left him alone in the cornfields.

"I can work hard," he assured her, gripping the phone tight in his hands. "I promise."

📱

HE'D ALWAYS WANTED TO GO to New York. The city—not where his Aunt Maybelle lived, up in Wayne County. Aunt Maybelle ran a farm not much different from his pa's, so even though she lived in New York, whenever he saw pictures of her house he always thought, *That's no different than Texas.*

The city was the real New York. Bright Broadway lights, the air smelling of car exhaust and street food instead of cow manure, and people who weren't judged or afraid to be who they wanted to be. Couples made out on street corners and let their cupped hands and long arms sway across the length of sidewalks, blocking passersby. If you looked closely you could see men holding hands with other men, and if you looked even closer, men who were not really men, men who dressed like women on the outside to justify how they felt on the inside. Ryan's pa called them "sick," said that they were "even worse than the faggots"; but Ryan called them brave. To him, they were even more real than the men who felt that their balls and cocks were home.

That was the New York he dreamed of.

Instead, he'd only be touching ground in the Promised Land—hopping off one bus, the third of four, just to get on another to make the final five-hour trek up to Wayne County. As he sank into the plush fabric of the final coach bus, the exhaustion of the previous two days finally settling into his stiff and heavy shoulders, there went his dreams of plays and nights filled with clubs and speaking to handsome strangers. He'd go back to being a poor farm boy who everyone hated, headed up to Wayne County because he was in his aunt's debt.

Because he was into fairy princess shit.

☐

THE NEW YORK SUN WAS as unforgiving as the one in Texas, and Ryan could feel his buzzed head perspiring and frying beneath its heat. Aunt Maybelle had allowed him the luxury of a shower and his first home-cooked meal in days before she sent him right back to work, where his hands "at least could be put to good use." Ryan hadn't told her what he had done that made his pa kick him out of the house, and Aunt Maybelle hadn't asked. All she had wanted—all without saying—was for him to make himself useful, and to keep any of "those faggot thoughts" where they belonged: inside his head.

He was back to being covered in sweat, but at least the scent was his own; the smell of the stale Greyhound bus had been washed down the shower drain. Ryan dabbed at his moist forehead with the hem of his white undershirt. A light breeze passed over his exposed abdomen, sending the hairs of his happy trail to attention. When he dropped the fabric from his face, he caught the eye of another farmhand from across the field, whose gaze appeared to linger on Ryan. The man's eyes were dipped just enough to avoid full contact with Ryan's, but not low enough to be aimed at the ground. Ryan followed the man's gaze, past his curled lips, to realize the man was eyeing the bare, damp skin of his torso.

Ryan couldn't help but smile back, his expression mirroring the farmhand's, a dull ache spreading through his chest. So this was what it felt like to be desired, to be looked at with anything other than disgust.

Pulling his hand away from his hair, he scratched his clammy, sweat-soaked palm with the tips of his fingers. The dead skin of his scalp caked beneath his fingernails, and Ryan could feel the faintest specks of gritty glitter, the pink and purple flecks reflecting back at him from where they had ingrained themselves in the lines of his palm, under his nails.

Evocative. Haunting.

Never to wash away. ⬛

tara isabella burton

TARA ISABELLA BURTON's work on religion, culture, and place can be found at *National Geographic*, *Al Jazeera America*, *Smithsonian Magazine*, *BBC*, *Atlantic*, and more. Her fiction has appeared or is forthcoming in Tor.com, *PANK*, *Shimmer*, and more. She is the winner of the *Spectator*'s 2012 Shiva Naipaul Memorial Prize for travel writing. She has recently completed her first novel.

HERE IN AVALON

I t was the last of those such nights.

All summer, we had walked the streets—our feet aching, our blisters breaking open, our makeup running down our face, and us ignoring them all. Our perfume smelled like cigarettes. Our cigarettes smelled like incense. All summer we had walked alone, together, whiskey-tainted shadows appearing in our corners one after another: in jaundiced vestibules of ninety-nine-cent pizzerias; in the neon stairwells of Saint Mark's.

Youth kept us wandering. We'd come down from 96th Street at a quarter to eleven, walked to Houston and then to Delancey and although even the most riotous bars were closed we had not stopped, nor even turned around, because to turn around would be to declare the night half over and this we would not do. We reveled in so many spotlights: the rainbow skein of black, oil-skimmed puddles, the reflective iteration of the traffic-lights, the twinkling of the Chrysler Building with all its approximated stars, the clock by the Flatiron building we had once drunkenly taken for the moon, to which Isadora had once addressed a pirouetted soliloquy in her armor, for which Julian had cut a pink lock of his hair and burned it with a cigarette-lighter as sacrifice, to which we'd all addressed an echolalia of worshipful epithets before Rex had noticed the black, arrow-ticking hand.

Every dawn for a hundred dawns we'd done this.

We would never do this again.

Tomorrow: Isadora, with her family, upstate before college, back for Thanksgiving, if then. Next week: Julian, summer receptionist gig at his uncle's dentistry practice in Crown Heights, his hair dyed black again. On the twenty-third: Rex and his mother to Italy for two weeks—he was the only one of us who could afford to go to Italy—and we envied him and hated him and pretended to think him foolish for daring to compare some shattered emperors to this.

By September: only me.

By then the shine of the moon and the smell of the stars and the neon-spiked reflections in the gutter would be gone.

I could not think about it now.

Julian took my arm and glided with me down Morton Street, stopping only to vault over postboxes.

"Extraordinary, isn't it?" We had come to the Christopher Street Pier and Isadora was swaying in the moonlight, nodding at the 10th Avenue garages, the strip clubs, the skyscrapers beyond, shaking down her hair. "For someone else, though," she said. "Not for me."

I could not look at her. One look at her Botticelli face and her pre-Raphaelite shoulders and the gold flecks in her eyes and I would start crying, or turn into salt.

"I belong somewhere else." She stretched her toes out toward the water. "Renaissance Rome?" She looked up at me.

I couldn't say anything. "Montmartre, 1899. Vienna, 1910. On the Ringstrasse. I'm taking German this fall. *Zweig, von Rezzori, and Viennese Melancholy: 1880–1914.*" She gave a little laugh. "*Mein Gott!*"

She took out some paper cups from her bag; she filled them with bergamot tea from a thermos and the Frangelico she'd secreted in a flask in one of the pockets; she stumbled and all I could think was how the world reeled with possibility at her feet.

"No," she said. "I don't belong here."

She passed around the glasses.

"And none of you do, either."

She squeezed my hand. She smiled at me, and then I half-thought she would ask me to come with her, to stow away in her car trunk for half a summer and live on apple cores under her dormitory bed for four years more. I would have done it.

"To love! *Damen. Herren. Enfants!*" Her voice rang on the water.

We raised our glasses.

"To never growing old."

"To never growing old."

We drank our tea, sweet and sick with liqueur, and I couldn't finish it so I poured the rest of mine into Isadora's cup, and she laughed and kissed the side of my forehead and said, *See? This is why I love you.*

Then it was dawn. Then we turned around.

I don't remember how we got to Delancey Street, or what we said in the interim. I remember that I was wearing Julian's blazer—velvet and too big for me—and that Rex needed Julian and Isadora to stop him from falling over an overturned garbage can, and that an aria hummed on Isadora's heart-shaped lips as we slumped him into a taxi and gave the driver his address. I remember Isadora's last pirouette in front of the all-night diner; I remember the two of them vanishing behind the turnstiles of the F train and I remember with all clarity the finality of the knowledge that I would not and never would kiss her.

"Come visit me in Vermont!"

It was the last thing Isadora ever said to me.

I told them I wanted to walk to the 6. I'd lied.

The truth was, the air still smelled like their cigarettes, like incense. I wanted to stand in it, like an invalid in a baker's shop, and breathe it all in until it was part of me, until it was gone.

That night I walked in circles. I visited places we'd been together—the crosswalk just north of Union Square where Isadora had told us about her first kiss and re-enacted it, all Shakespeare couplets and dead faints, on the back of Julian's hand; the section of the High Line where Julian had once done somersaults from the park benches, scattering tourists like pigeons, and where Rex had adjusted his spectacles so meticulously before letting himself applaud.

"Isadora is the poetess," he'd said, "And Julian is the acrobat. And *I* am the arbiter of taste." He had said nothing to me.

When I reached our old tea shop I cried, and with fog in my eyes and viscous hazelnut still on my lips, I headed steadfastly downtown, down alleyways, as if the city were a great unending thing of dragons, and any rivers or borders I'd known were lies.

I was always the last to leave. That was my great skill.

I heard the music before anything else: a chord that shuddered an electric pulse within me, and it was only after I'd stopped to grip the railing and sob that I heard her voice, or the words.

Come, lonely traveler
and lonely, make your home
when your feet give up their wand'ring
and your soul can no longer roam

The steps vibrated and behind the door—half-submerged by pavement, in the basement of an old brown-sided tenement—I saw a neon slice.

Come dry your tears upon me
wipe your eyes upon my breast
I will give you, lonely, comfort
I will give you wand'ring, rest

It never occurred to me that I had a choice.

I took the steps two at a time; I flung open the door. I followed her down another flight of stairs and then another, and then at the base of another stair, so deep I knew we would not see daylight, she was waiting for me.

Butterflies fluttered on her eyelids; peacock feathers twined from her ears in a braid that reached her feet. Her sequins were white; they shimmered—synchronized—in stages, so that first her breasts shone and then her shoulders, and then when she moved, light fell upon the spikes at her feet. Her lips were red; her hair was long; her words were lost in an electric eruption of sound. She wore wings.

When she sang it bore through me; when she swayed it undid me. Around me, in the darkness, cigarettes glowed like fireflies, and we were all dancing, and linking our arms, and making with our bodies one unbreakable chain.

She fixed her eyes on me:

> *Come, lonely traveler*
> *and lonely, make your home*
> *when your feet give up their wand'ring*
> *and your soul can no longer roam*

Her music shook me until my bones shattered like champagne flutes. She sang a song for travelers, another for lovers, one for pilgrims. A pair of redheaded twins danced with a man with discolored eyes; a woman with Renaissance-wild hair had a clover birthmark; when she came closer I saw she had applied it herself with makeup and in the sweat of dawn it had come slightly smudged.

And the woman in white kept singing:

> *Come dry your tears upon me*
> *wipe your eyes upon my breast*

She choked out her heart over the microphone. Then she stopped, she smiled, raised the microphone like a glass in greeting, and then kissed her fingers and spread them out to me.

"Child," the one with the birthmark took my hand in hers; she pressed them to her lips and stained them. "This isn't a place for tears."

She took out a pencil from her purse of alligator skin. She drew something on my lower lip that smelled like bergamot.

"You won't stop dancing, will you?"

"Never."

It was all I knew how to say.

We danced.

The twins were on either side of me; they linked hands and created a chain; the girl took my left and the boy my right—at least, I thought they had, but when I looked up again their positions were reversed, and as the music grew louder I felt it in all the deepest parts of my body: in my wrist, in my collarbones, in my throat.

I kept searching for the woman in white; there were so many of us in the crowd, now, that I could not see her. There was no space but the space between my hands and hers; there was no time but the syncopation of beats.

Then silence.

Then our bodies parted, and the woman in white was surrounded by so many feathers, whiter still than she was, and nobody moved but she stood with her arms outstretched, her neck cygnet-long, her eyes invisible behind the starlike glimmer of her lashes.

Nobody said anything. I looked around, wildly, for some object, some trinket, some sacrifice I could lay down before her, and it was only when the woman with the birthmark pushed me forward did I understand.

I fell to my knees; she made me rise. She took me in, close enough that I could see her eyes were as pale as her wings, and I have never seen a woman or a sunrise or a city street as beautiful as the single fleck of blue in them.

"You're new?"

"Yes."

"How did you find us?"

"I was lonely. I heard the music."

"Will you stay for the last song?"

"I'll stay as long as it takes," I said.

She smiled. "We're going late tonight."

"I don't care," I said. "I have nowhere else to go."

"I know," she said, and kissed me. Her lips burned my

forehead and I let my head rest between her breasts. "Stay as long as you need to."

I stayed. I danced. She had dried my tears where she had touched them, and so in the fury of my joy I stretched out my hands to the twins, the woman with the birthmark, the aurora straggles coming in one at a time with the same loneliness stamped on them, and I drew clovers above their lips, and comforted them when they wept.

She sang songs for marriages, songs for the births of children, for the death of dear friends, elegies and laments. She sang songs of great learning, and great invention, and of the wisdom of the men who have lived long enough to see the world start once more from the very beginning.

The last song was a lullaby.

By then the drummer and the guitarist had gone, and the only instrument she had was a music box, and as the little dancer spiraled I swayed, and as she slowed I sank, and by the time her voice faded into silence I too had fallen asleep, curled up on a pile of tawny mink coats and leopard-skin pillows.

When I woke I was alone. The bar was empty; the equipment was gone; shafts of sunlight fell across the floor in streams.

So this was morning.

I blinked my eyes and rubbed their corners and emerged, one shaking step at a time, onto the crosswalk of two unfamiliar streets. I knew none of the signs. I only let my feet take me back the way I'd come, along avenues whose names I did not know but whose shape I recognized, until at last I recognized Park Avenue with its awnings lit all gold by the intensity of summer.

Then I hailed a taxi—a green that was almost violet, I thought, or maybe it was just my contact lenses in the light—and I gave him my mother's address, and he looked at me strangely but sped uptown anyway, and once we were moving I began, at last, to cry.

I told myself it was better to smile through my tears. Better to tell the driver to turn back, or at least stop him long enough for me to tell him about Julian's somersaults and Rex's emperors and Isadora's pagan sacrifices to the moon, about the redheaded twins and the clovers and the woman whose feathers were all white, so white, and who had kissed me where it had burned.

It was the tears that made me uncertain.

When I first caught a glimpse of myself in his rearview mirror, and saw that my hair was white and that wrinkles lined my face and that where she had kissed me there was a crescent mole sprouting one or two salt-colored hairs, I thought it was only that I'd been crying.

I dabbed them with a tissue and looked again into the mirror and waited for my own face to appear again. It took me all the way to 59th Street to realize it would not.

It was there that, shaking, I stopped him and paid my fare, and then walked out into the wide open city, between buildings I did not recognize, by the East River and then down and then up again, until I grew breathless and my bones started to ache, until I could not walk any further and settled down on a bench where the Christopher Street Pier used to be, to wait. ⬛

katherine sloan

KATHERINE SLOAN is a freelance writer and editor from Virginia. She received her Master's Degree in English with a concentration in Creative Writing in 2012 from Longwood University. This is her second piece published by Three Rooms Press. She is currently writing mostly nonfiction, though her poetry has been published by Mystery Island Publications and she has read at the Bowery Poetry Club. Recently she freelanced for the writer Rick Moody. She lives in New York City. Follow her on Instagram under sloankatherine or on Twitter @Katherinesloan8.

BECAUSE YOU WERE UNDER THIRTY

He died in the building where you were living when you first came to New York. There were smells (he wasn't found for days), fumigation, and only glimpses of the room where it happened on the fourth floor as you passed down the stairwell. You didn't realize then that mortality would be something that entered your thoughts more and more as you started a life in New York. He was just an old man who had a heart attack: no tragedy. You were just a young girl of twenty-four not wanting to let on that death could happen to someone who hadn't even lived yet. That would've been the real tragedy: buying the farm just after you left it.

Manhattan turned into Queens; frustration and sexual tension turned into half-hearted attempts at fucking. Blow jobs with no ending: no denouement. Winter turned into spring with amazing blossoms that made your eyes light up. You met a guy who called your pussy a flower: he wanted your dewy pink flower. Another disappointment. "Talk dirty to me; tell me a filthy story and don't skimp on the details" (how did your friend know to talk like that that—how did she have *all* that experience?).

Jobs and interviews turned into self-loathing (how could they not have wanted *you?*). Fancy people *loved* you! You were one of the exceptional ones: not a bourgeois. No, certainly not. The one who could turn a detail on its head and it suddenly became the funniest joke they had ever heard. You were the one with the hair, the cleavage, the really good designer knockoffs.

And then a year or so passed and those spring blossoms stared you dead in the face again. Everything bloomed and a fever set in. First it started with the one who wasn't staying for long. The one with the convoluted accent that lost its charm rather quickly. Nothing but kisses on the street and in the subway. Your lipstick was smeared across his face. Then there was the one who said (in a diner on the Upper West Side) that he liked to fuck other men's wives as they watched. And then he didn't return *your* phone calls. *L'amour, l'amour—how do we live without it?* There was the friend to whom you said "I love you" but that was so long ago. He took your youth for granted and didn't understand that he had just won the jackpot.

You gossiped to your girlfriends; they said, "We work in a shi shi boutique. We sell Cosabella and we talk about guys. *Call* him!" Another accent came along and it was disarmingly elegant. It told you to take off your knickers, to lick his balls before he could come. He said, "You're half my age. That's *very* good." The melodic voice became less charming and your supermodel friend said, "CUT BAIT! Alcoholism is a disease! Worse than a *heart attack!*" on a crosstown bus. You learned that buying beer at the corner

deli in the morning to nurse his hangover could be a deal
breaker. It didn't matter how much he loved your "glorious
round bottom."

Then there was the young one who sounded like a real,
live text message: "Nice to meet you IRL." "What's IRL?" you
asked. You were very young but couldn't talk *that* young. This
wasn't quite as bad as the has-been Lothario who only used
technology in order to break up with you. The tip that kept
reverberating in your head: a vibrator is a useful invention,
too. It may even be a handier technology than e-mail.

There was the one who drank too much, the one who
didn't drink at all because of an allergy, the one who spoke
in AA jargon, the one who only drank too much when you
actually wanted him to call, and the one who only liked you
when he was drunk. Alcohol played a huge role in people's
dating lives in New York: the surplus of it or the lack of it. It
was the most harmful drug because it disappointed you
more than any other. You knew you could walk into any
mediocre art opening in Chelsea and get free, cheap white
or red wine. You decorated your walls with free postcards
from galleries (this was only acceptable when you were in
your twenties. Over thirty requires the purchase of a frame).

Suddenly, you were a member of the dating club. It was
something you had always heard about but were never able
to join until New York. It was easy when you were young to
flirt; you could just say "I'm twenty-six!" When you're under
thirty, everything is misconstrued as flirting. You took it to
the next level and became obnoxious: you balanced a business card on your breast before handing it to a prospective
date. You never forgot where you first lived when you moved
to New York City, where the old man died and wasn't found

for days and you thought that seemed almost glamorous. You came to think of it as something that wasn't even note-worthy. You lost your grandmother and your mother lay with her dead body before the ambulance came. She had a small cut on her lip where she fell. That was real and you knew it, even at twenty-six. New York was just dress-up, make believe, pretend compared to that.

You missed the going-away party for the girl who was leaving New York because of a rent-hike and bedbugs; somehow it didn't seem so important. You dreaded summer and wanted to revel in spring but you felt like wilting rather than blossoming, wanting to live but afraid of "withering in the bud." The dying petals littered the cars like pink con-fetti; you loved the petals from the Kwanzan cherry trees. You only bought carnations because they reminded you of Gloria Swanson, were cheap, and you craved glamour; they frilled up the apartment and, if you didn't want to stay in, there was always something going on in the city because you were young. This was a consolation: a reminder of the mas-querade. You could dress up again and feel good about your-self—but that seems like a twenty-something notion now, like the charade that was and always will be New York.   ◻

▶ YOU WERE JUST
A YOUNG GIRL
OF TWENTY-FOUR
NOT WANTING
TO LET ON THAT
DEATH COULD
HAPPEN TO
SOMEONE WHO
HADN'T EVEN
LIVED YET.

carolyn a drake

A Jersey Shore native, **CAROLYN A. DRAKE** is a writer and editor with a focus in pharmaceutical writing and an interest in fiction. She is currently a Promotional Review Editor with Bristol-Myers Squibb. Formerly a freelance writer, her articles have been featured on HCPlive.com, for which she was a regular contributor. "Pill Pusher" is Carolyn's first short work of fiction to be selected for publication. At present, she is completing her first full-length work, a supernatural-themed novel immersed in the world of pharmacy. Follow her on Twitter @Carolyn_A_Drake.

PILL
PUSHER

Around 12:43 p.m., I realize that I have made a $70,000 mistake.

"Ma'am," my voice strains above the rush-hour din of the Walgreens pharmacy, my tired lips no longer capable of mimicking a faux-friendly customer service smile, "you have to stand over here—"

"I've been waiting for fifteen minutes!" Bug-eyed Coach sunglasses shade her from narrow eyebrow to cheek, but her impatient foot tapping has already sent the message: this is an important lady, who has fantastically important things to tend to today.

Such vital things, I think with a glance around the crowded pharmacy queue, *like grocery shopping at Whole Foods and prepping for a PTA meeting smackdown.*

"We didn't realize you weren't being helped," I reply with all the patience I have left after a nonstop three-hour onslaught. *And I didn't realize that getting a pharmacy degree would damn me to a life in retail, pushing pills for soccer moms and their ADHD-riddled children.*

But that's not all! Billy Mays's voice interrupts my thoughts with orgasmic enthusiasm. *You'll also get a crushing sense of inadequacy for being a legalized drug dealer, feeding addictions for Cialis and Zoloft and Oxycodone! In addition, you'll get $70,000 in student loans! Not to mention a 12 percent interest rate, starting six months after graduation! That's a lifetime of unfulfillment and debt for six years of education! What a bargain!*

"Well, I've been *standing* here!" Bug Eyes spreads her arms wide and waves them, and I am reminded of a toddler on the threshold of a tantrum.

"The line is actually over there," I point to a teenage girl with worried eyes—*Plan B or Yaz*, I mentally wager—shifting from foot to foot behind a gangly young man in long sleeves and a beanie who shoots me a manic grin and waves when my eyes slide over him. *Heroin addict, will ask for diabetic needles for his "grandma." I'll bet ten to one he offers to get me a cup of coffee while he waits, because he's just such a nice guy.*

Bug Eyes issues the line a dismissive glance and turns up her nose. "How am I supposed to know where the line is? You're not doing anything, right?" She interrupts as I open my mouth to explain how lines work: "Why can't you just grab my prescription?"

Self-entitled bitch. "I'm in the middle of something," I hold up the hypodermic needle and flu shot vaccine bottle for the flirtatious silver-haired gentleman one of the technicians ushered to the clinical waiting room five minutes earlier, "but if you could just come over here and wait just a moment—"

"I *have* been waiting!" The woman's voice rises over the decibel of annoyance to irrational anger. "*You* haven't been paying attention!"

My eyes flicker to the group of people milling around in front of the pharmacy counter; no one makes eye contact. Customers waiting for their prescriptions pretend to check their phones while observing the exchange between irate customer and jaded millennial pharmacist from their peripheral vision. *Everyone loves a goddamned train wreck, after all.*

I glance around the pharmacy for assistance; the pharmacy manager is on the phone wrestling with an insurance agency over a Coumadin co-pay, and the two technicians scurry between the drive-through and the ever-ringing phone like ants shadowed by a large boot. They take no interest in the situation unraveling at the counter.

I'll have to handle this.

Bloated soccer mom who consumes Lean Cuisines, goes to Pilates classes, and takes placebo-effect dietary supplements because Oprah told her to, I diagnose. *Prognosis: Incurable.*

Just get her out of here and move on to the drug addict.

My teeth clench as I swivel and slide the bottle back into the fridge, disposing of the unused needle in the Sharps bin beneath the counter before turning to Bug Eyes. "What can I get for you?"

Her mouth twitches in triumph, and she steps forward to thrust the blue prescription paper across the counter. I inspect the scrawled chicken scratch. Amoxicillin. Of course. *Her kid has a cold—obviously far more important than anyone else's prescription.*

"This is for an eight-year-old?" I ask.

"Yes, my daughter."

"She's okay with swallowing large pills?"

"No, it's supposed to be a liquid."

"Okay, it says pills here."

"Can you switch it?"

"I actually have to call the doctor."

"You've got to be kidding me."

"Sorry, we can't legally alter prescriptions without—"

"Oh, this is horseshit!"

Blood thumps in my ears. Everyone is staring. "Ma'am—"

"This is ridiculous! We've been loyal customers for years, and this has been the most *appalling* treatment!"

"Ma'am, it's not Walgreens," I try to explain, "it's—" *the law*, but the words are cut off before I can finish.

"You know what? Fine!" she squawks, ripping her sunglasses off. Eye to eye, she fixes me with a vile glare. "Call the damn doctor! His office closes at one, so hurry it up or you're going to miss him! And for the record, I *will* be calling corporate to lodge a complaint about your treatment of this entire situation!"

White heat sears my skin. My ears thrum. The pressure of the morning boils over.

"Go for it!" I roar back, slamming the prescription on the counter. "In the meantime, can I get back to my goddamn job?"

A horrified silence cuts through the murmuring store. Bug Eyes stares, jaw slack, stunned, but mercifully mute.

I swallow. "Thank you!" Without waiting for a retort, I turn my burning face away from the counter and start punching in the last name on the prescription into the computer system. My fingers shake as I struggle to type. I am vaguely aware of my coworkers' alarmed gazes and the hushed whispers between the techs, but I refuse to meet their eyes, convinced they'll be able to see the broken thread of nerves behind my own.

Went too far, lost it, snapped, and now I'll be fired, lose my job only two years out of school and burn the retail bridge forever. I'll have to move out of state to find work, all because of my stupid, stupid mouth, because I couldn't keep control.

You know what? A fiercer, embittered voice snarls over the meek, panicked one in my head. *GOOD. Fire me. Burn this bridge. I'll find something, anything else. Anything is better than bottling self-help for self-pitying idiots who wouldn't know true sickness if it crawled into their evening cocktail. So fucking go for it. Make my day, punk.*

Resolved to update my CV tonight over a glass (bottle) of wine, I open the record for Bug Eyes, searching for her doctor's phone number. In the upper right-hand corner, however, the little yellow folder that reads NOTES catches my eye.

A sudden urge for some validation in light of my unprofessional reaction grips me. Eager to see what previous pharmacists have to say about rude ol' Bug Eyes, I click open the "comments" section of the profile.

As I scan the comments, I feel cold fingers clench around my ribcage.

> 3/13 Patient had questions about daughter's first round of Dasatinib. Recommended talking to primary care about Zofran for the nausea.

> 6/13 Patient had questions about Dexamethasone side effects on daughter during treatment (6).

> 9/13 Needed to call primary care to confirm Percocet refill.

> 2/15 Patient's daughter recently left hospital, had questions about second round of treatment, effect on antibiotics.

The pharmacy, although bustling again with activity, falls silent as I absorb what I've read.

Zofran for the nausea, steroids for the bloating, Percocet for the pain. . . .

Dasatinib. Leukemia. *Damn.*

I yank my eyes away from the computer screen, and they are drawn to the puffy-faced woman glaring at me from across the counter, indignant. I suddenly notice wrinkles well beyond those appropriate for a thirty-something. She's not much older than me—maybe ten years.

Ten years ago I decided to go to school for pharmacy.

I fold the prescription and jot down the doctor's number on the back of it. He immediately clears the prescription. I type up the label, pour the amoxicillin syrup into a prescription bottle, and turn back to the counter.

"Here you go." The woman wordlessly grabs the bag and starts to turn, but I hold on to the bag. She turns back to me.

"Try bland white rice for nausea," I say, "in addition to the Zofran. It helped a lot with my stomach ulcer."

For a moment, her brow hardens, as if she's about to scream at me again, but then it softens for the first time. The lines around her taut mouth smooth.

"Thank you." Flustered, she flounders for a beat before stuttering, "I-I shouldn't have yelled before, I . . . I . . ."

"Don't worry about it. Happens to us all." And I smile genuinely for the first time today.

I let go of the bag and she stays motionless for a moment, swaying. Then she nods and briskly turns, retreating to the front of the store.

I watch her until she disappears into an aisle smelling of BenGay and Neosporin. Then I turn to face the crowd of customers waiting for me.

Force a smile, I remind myself, and struggle but manage to do just so. "Can I help the next person?" ◻

ifra asad

IFRA ASAD is originally from Karachi, Pakistan. She did her undergraduate studies in Creative Writing from Franklin and Marshall College in Lancaster, PA, and her MA in Comparative Literatures of Africa, Asia, and the Middle East from SOAS, University of London. Her dissertation focused on late-twentieth-century Urdu short stories, and her fiction has appeared in *Bicycle Review*. Since then, her interests have turned to activism; she currently works at Women Living Under Muslim Laws, a transnational solidarity network. This is her first publication at Three Rooms Press.

THE OSTRICH
EFFECT

O n Tuesday evening, after I got off from work, I decided I was going to spend the next year of my life underground. The thought came to me as I descended the A train steps outside a grimy 8th Avenue, people bumping into me with the fatal urgency of emergency wards. Cigarette smoke when I didn't ask for it. Never when I did. Flyers overflowing my purse. I thought, as my blistered feet click-clacked down the gum-pocked, pee-stained stairs, that for the next year, I am going to live on these trains.

And why not? It was a sudden, impulsive thought, the kind that comes to you late on sleepless nights when your sides ache from all the tossing and turning. On the eve of my twenty-third birthday, one side of the balance tipping with the weight of little green baggies and lighters, the other with The Boss, calling me into his office, telling me: *take a seat, we should talk.* And, I thought, hand bumping along the rust-coated railing, it isn't a bad decision. People do it all the time. Drop out of the earth and disappear, live right under everyone's nose without anyone ever knowing. I'll live underground, and stay there with the fierce insistence of an ostrich until the danger overhead— the disappointingly misted-over silhouette of the Empire State Building as it snows; the grimy gray slush of February sidewalks; the sallow, reproachful, domineeringly authoritative face waiting for me every 9 a.m., shoving a pile of papers my way to route around a cramped haze of cubicles—until all of that has passed. Keep my head in the sand until I no longer have to, until it has all gone on and blown over without me. Sleep off the incessant nagging thoughts. Block out the demands of sudden adulthood.

So I did. I moved underground.

Admittedly, there was an adjustment process. Unfamiliar at first. The growling cloud of nine-to-five foot traffic replaced by the roar of hurtling, decades-old trains. Weaving in and out of people meant something different now, as I no longer rushed my way to rundown elevators at 9:02 a.m. But then, steadily, as we do with most things, I grew into it. The smoky grime snaking its way under my eyes, through my fingernails, into my bloodstream, as it filtered more and more into me everyday. Gradually, I began to develop a set routine. A steady cadence of wake-up-heres, go-to-sleep-theres. Avoid the MTA at Union Square; it's tourist-heavy. Stay alert at Canal Street; that's where the cops are. Up around Harlem, on the West Side, you're safe. Maybe stick to Bronx-side trains, away from Wall Street and its sea of suffocating gray suits, watches that cost my skinny limbs, shoes an alligator somewhere died for. Avoid the L— with its flannel-clad, pencil-mustachioed, exclusive-and- unwelcome-club-member kids—like the plague.

And I began to develop this routine, to hone and refine it till all the kinks were ironed out. Like for food. I would quietly nick Subway sandwiches and Wendy's leftovers from people's bags. Sometimes, I would bump into them on purpose: make them drop their things; snatch their food and run. And this would happen often. They would chase after me and I would snicker away as I seeped through subway stops and secret passageways until they could never find me again. I would find a perfect hole somewhere, and I would crack open my findings and revel in them. Like Aladdin, after escaping the Baghdad police. Swinging through wooden scaffolding with a cartoon grin on his face, lively mischief bandaging up deep-seated fears. Cracking apart a slice of bread to enjoy with his pet monkey, because after all, that's just another Wednesday.

For company: the usual suspects. The homeless. The needy. The occasional limbless beggars, the subway performers, the meth heads with no idea where they were or what they were saying to anyone. Voices booming after years of training, because it took a booming voice to land petty change, empty plastic cups rattling with nickels and dimes and throats scratching after years of screams. *My name's Dolores Something. I'm a diabetic. I'm hungry. Please, won't you help me out?* Pause five seconds. *My name's Dolores Something. I'm a diabetic. I'm hungry. Please, won't you help me out?* Pause five seconds.

And then, the local hangouts I made. In Astoria, for example, I would join the hunched-over woman on the floor, her bulging, frog-like, and eerily vacant eyes staring blankly ahead, skin gathered in folds around her eyebrows. Teeth silently gnashing and un-gnashing. I would say things like, *Ain't life the dumps*. We would sit there, silently, reveling in what we didn't have in common, our respective cups next to us competing in inches of coins. On Lexington Avenue I would throw back a stolen beer with the stumbling alcoholic who sometimes sat on the bench, muttering to himself, *They're better with not letting in food on the train in England. I haven't had a meal in days. But hey, I'm still here. I'm still alive, I think. Ain't that right, girl?* And I would clink my beer against his and say something like, *ain't that the truth*. And he would say, *Mm. Amen. You know how it is*. Or up on 125th street, snaking through the 1, I would join the raving man with the honey-mashed hair on end, one shoe off and banging against the wall as he would yell, *I will stab every one of you motherfuckers if you look at me. Don't look at me.* Banging his shoe, *Don't look at me, imma stab all of you.* Stopping every few minutes to pick at his hair, then lick it off his fingers. Sometimes I would gingerly join him in what he was doing, during his brief and rare spells of lucidity. I'd find things in his hair for him, make his nitpicking easier. It would become our friendly activity—me picking his hair, him keeping me company.

As for boredom: well, there were the trains, and they never got old. I spent the next months alternating from a Bronx-bound crowd, to a Queens-bound troupe, a Brooklyn-bound bevy, and the Manhattan-dwelling folks stepping off, stepping on, stepping off, stepping on, a steady, sheep-like cadence that never slowed down and never sped up. Unwanted Tetris pieces in God's moments of idle procrastination. I made, as I waited at the edge of the platform—*Ladies and gentlemen, for your safety, please stand away from the platform edge*—poetry, sheer poetry out of fragments of conversations. Sociological studies, haikus, relationships forming and falling, everything. I observed it all; all in a little notebook, with fingers growing grubbier every day, nails that started to peel off around month seven. I wrote these things down, planning for eventual emergence, hair the size of a beehive, a warm stench of urine encompassing me. I would hold up this container of truth, I'd think. The sheer truth. That's what this notebook would hold. The ultimate, omniscient truth about all of human behavior, observed and lived from someone who knows it, because they spent a year on trains eavesdropping for clues. All the questions we have ever had about ourselves, answered through fragments caught from other people. Every overwhelmed moment about who to suddenly be. Every pondered-over thought about what-else-did-we-expect? Every subdued answer to what next? Every unforeseen fork on every unforeseen road. Now we would have the answers.

Like that, I spent the last few months. Riding and riding the subways, ending up at various parts of the map, my brain a swirl of buzzers and automated messages, passengers banging into each other, the occasional *Ladies and gentlemen, we are looking for a missing child, last seen on 51st Street, contact the MTA authorities if*—

And I have spent about a year here, and I might spend years here, surrounded by this musty odor, these spit-covered benches, the rattling of trains to mark the passage of intervals. The furious roar of the E train; the orangey comfort of the BDFM; the bourgeois sensibility of the 456; the ambiguous diversity of the 123.

I think, in a little while, when I have gotten from it what I need, when I'm done not thinking about what I'm trying to avoid, when my twelve months are entirely up, I'll gingerly scrape my way toward the steps, whatever steps, whatever station of whatever borough I happen to be in. I'll inch toward them like a child being nudged toward a clown, or a house cat toward an open backyard door. And crowds will cheer and ribbons will be cut, and I'll re-emerge, changed, revitalized, new. And everything will become fresh and I'll take that first shower and none of the old layers will matter anymore, and everything I left up there will have dissipated into New York gutters and foggy August evenings. And my place in that office in Midtown will make more sense, and my climb will suddenly be easier, and I'll have skipped all the growing pains and the incessant questions I'm tired of being asked and of asking myself and days will no longer feel like a swamp waiting to be waded through. And I will scrunch up my eyes and look to the sun and nod my head in that promising gesture they make in the movies—that gesture that says, *Now we are here. Now there is promise. Now things will change.*

But that's for another time. My train has pulled up, and I have looped an arm around a sweating man's bald head to reach an inch of the metal bar behind him.

For now, I intend to just stay on these trains. Content under the sand, with the orange seats my temporary throne, the blue ones my comfortable bed, as the train hurtles on and on, under the ground, rumbling on while millions of unknowing feet carry on their dainty little businesses everyday overhead.

Because, the thing is, I don't think I'm done here yet. ◘

constance renfrow

CONSTANCE RENFROW is a New York-based writer and editor. She is the lead editor for Three Rooms Press and a freelance editor and writing coach. She recently launched a monthly open mic series at the Merchant's House Museum, where she is a volunteer graphic designer and costumed performer. Her fiction and poetry have appeared in such places as *Cabildo Quarterly*, *Denim Skin*, *Petrichor Machine*, *Restless*, and *Two Cities Review*, and her articles have been featured on DIY MFA and LitroNY, among others. A lover of nineteenth-century literature, she's currently completing a three-volume governess novel, her first full-length work.

THE EDGE OF
HAPPINESS

Robert's edges are the first I see. It's during his gallery opening they appear. At first there is nothing, only hanging frames and oversized abstracts, and then of a sudden, someone is mouthing words to him, is pointing at the painting he'd once felt himself unable to finish, and Robert begins to glow. A blurred white border that clings to his skin and isolates him from the crowds circling the room.

Walking home to the Harlem brownstone will take so much longer tonight, because Chelsea galleries are farther south than the antique store desk on the Upper East Side, where I point to Edwardian sapphires and vintage chiaroscuro. Most customers already know their provenance; they tell me I pronounce Lladró wrong, that of course this brooch is Retro not Art Deco. I don't tell them that their noses are dull, their eyelids inelegant, that they could have never inspired the masterpieces on their walls. Still, it's noon to six, enough money for rent, time to draw before and after and when business is slow. I'll be back there tomorrow; back to sketching the visages that scowl in period oil paint—over and over on recycled 8½ x 11s—each time the door closes on patrons who care nothing for this century's art.

But this evening I'm walking, because the apartment's too cold and a Metrocard swipe is now $2.75, and besides, my sketchbook has stayed empty for weeks. No matter that New York is known for its many faces, its slouching beauties; they keep crossing before the light turns green, keep staring down at phones and maps or into each other's eyes—I haven't even wanted to draw them.

On 9th Ave, I pass a young mother listening to her toddler shriek. As I get close, I see how her expression contorts at his pitch, and there around her, is an outline like Robert's, insubstantial and white. And when she picks up her kid, he finds his edges too. They merge together, become almost blinding, and I don't wait to see any more.

At 8th, so many leftover businessmen wander toward Penn Station, toward home and the LIRR—even though it's long past 5 p.m. Some have borders; other silhouettes stop at their suit jackets. I watch how one drops some dollars in the hat of the girl belting out show tunes under the overhang. Some amount poorer, he has edges now; some amount richer, she does not.

I cut east along 31st, wondering why I'm seeing these lights like auras, when a street psychic knocks at me between the lettering on her storefront. I turn back and she opens the door, stepping out into the darkness of the late-November evening.

"Hey, miss," she says, and I see how her edges are first hardly there and then flare white, sliding down her sweater and thighs, cascading from her shoulders in tandem with her curls. Against the black shadow of Madison Square Garden, her outline is eerie, or maybe just unearthly. I've passed city psychics enough to know their standard line— *Something is troubling you*—but instead what she says is, "I can tell you why you're seeing outlines. Why you don't have one."

For the first time I examine my hands, my jeans. She's right. I see only what's normal of me—freckles and too-fancy seams. She points to the writing on the glass. "A Tarot reading is only five dollars."

I say, "I don't need any faces on cards." I tell her I know what the future holds—I just want to know why I'm seeing outlines like bad reception, or shitty CGI. Like everyone's standing in front of a green screen but me.

She leans in close, her eyes the slate gray of pencil lead, and on her sweater I smell nicotine and spearmint. When she clutches my hand, her edges don't spill onto me. They touch my skin but never spread.

"Okay," I say, and she pulls me in past the door someone's painted to say: MISS CLEO, PSYCHIC READINGS.

The room is the size of a phone booth or a prison cell— what she tells me is her office. Prisms dangle from a mirror, a zodiac is pinned beside it, and she sits me at a table so small that our kneecaps collide. The walls are daubed with red.

I see the whiteness that surrounds her. The nothingness that outlines me.

"These edges," I say. "What are they?" Because the mother seemed unaware that she was trapped in translucence, and Robert did not know his was there to tell me how it feels. "Is it a sign of something?" I ask Miss Cleo. "Or does it hurt them to glow?" Or does it mean—and maybe this is what I want to be true—that they are lesser than I who have no edge, that they have taken the first path presented, settled for mediocrity, and now have only to wait and wait and wait for anything more.

I tear at the skin on the side of my hand, where ink and charcoal have long stained into the creases. But I'm the one waiting now.

She tells me to take three cards, and so I slide three from the deck. My palm holds them facedown against the table-cloth, their futures pressing into the fabric. Their pictures don't matter, their meanings. They've told me the same things before: a change soon, something you love will leave you, buy magical trinkets and be healed. Thirty dollars, just for you.

Her long fake nails, made of plastic and glue, scrape against my skin as she pulls the cards from under my hand. Taps them against the deck.

The Fool, Miss Cleo flips first. "New beginnings." She tells me I'm looking for something new to believe in that isn't cap-turing in ink the way people yearn at night in the city—their muscles straining, their bodies pausing, because the galleries have closed and even the bartenders have gone to sleep.

The Tower next, and I'm made to know that my dreams won't come true. That my castle in the air is crumbling, has broken into dust upon the salt waters below. That the antique store is draining away my soul's images, because of its out-of-date aesthetic and dreary faces that no longer hold any interest for me.

"Excuse me?" The words are stilted, rasping. I didn't tell her how I make rent, or what I moved to New York to do.

As she rubs her fingers down the corners of her lips, her

edges merge, spilling into the gaps caused by the move-
ment—still one continuous, ethereal outline. She says,
"That's what's in the cards."

I tell her this is bullshit, that none of this answers why outlines are emerging, surrounding the people who know
nothing about them—who don't feel the energy or see the
luminescence of their skin. I tell her I want to know where
my edges have gone, or if I ever had them.

Miss Cleo reaches for the final card, dropping her shoulders down, draping herself across the table. She looks at me
with those lustrous eyes through curls that have fallen across
her brow, that twine down her cheekbones and cover the fur-
rows in her skin. In the shadows the details hide. I think
then I will remember her tonight, when I'm back to crouching
on the floor, pen in hand, over an empty sketchbook page.

She says, "You know you flickered just now?" And her
fingernails pry up the Nine of Cups. The card of "yes" and
everything's possible.

I know every line, every pen stroke to render on the page
my sneer. To depict skepticism, scorn.

"You've had edges before—even right then." She does not
respond to how I laugh. "And you can have them again, but
you'll have to build up new dreams."

So no more of the ones gone down with the Tower. A new
job—and haven't I been considering a nine-to-five?—with
artistic coworkers and creative surroundings. But all I can
envision is how a street scene is established from skyscraper
to office building to the corner Starbucks I'll have to visit
each morning at eight forty-five.

"If you can do that," she says, "you will be incandescent."

So basically, out with the old, in with the new.

Prosaic.

Dull.

There's five dollars left in my pocket, and I drop the ink-smeared bill atop the Fool because that, at least, feels symbolic. I stand up—her elbow knocking into mine as she grabs at the cash. When I push my hand against the glass door, she says, with a voice dropped an octave, but still throaty and charged with the mystical, or maybe just smoke, "That's what you're seeing, you know. The outlines. They mean people are happy."

I make a noise somewhere between cough and cry. Remembering the mother with her raging brat and the businessman leaving the office far too late. "You mean they gave up, because that's what they were told to do!"

I don't mean to howl it.

Miss Cleo wraps her arms across her chest. Her outline grows like a shield, and she insists again, "It means they're happy *at the time*."

My shoulders go slack. So I'm seeing their joy. It emanates from their skin like body heat and can't be transferred through touch. If it did, I'd have been happy when Robert hugged me goodbye, when Miss Cleo took my hand outside the store.

Robert, then, was exultant. The street singer, I suppose, was not.

The psychic stares at me with her all-seeing eyes, and I drop my gaze down to the Tarot, still sprawled across the tablecloth—face up now, grinning at the inevitable. I don't want her to see how I had hoped to pity her—how I had thought, maybe, I was meant to.

"The outlines come and go," Miss Cleo says. "It's to be expected—good fortune is temporary." And then, after all:

"But I can show you how to use energy crystals to heal yourself so you'll glow too. Fifty dollars a set."

I shove my way out the door, leaving behind the gilt fiction of the psychic's façade, pushing in front of the cars and construction and tourists lost on the side roads. I see outlines—contented, joyful—on some, and some have only the broken slabs of their New York fantasies to keep them warm.

I think, maybe, tomorrow the cards will be right after all, and maybe then I'll search and apply, and cast out the dried-up and decaying faces on the walls. Maybe I will draw Miss Cleo's jawline, try to capture the way her profile gleams, so maybe my own will shine for a time. But the sky has long grown dark, and amidst the low beams and lights of city dusk, edges are glowing and their owners are radiant, and tonight it makes me sad.   ▢

RECENT AND FORTHCOMING BOOKS FROM THREE ROOMS PRESS

FICTION

Meagan Brothers
Weird Girl and What's His Name

Ron Dakron
Hello Devilfish!

Michael T. Fournier
Hidden Wheel
Swing State

Janet Hamill
Tales from the Eternal Café
(Introduction by Patti Smith)

Eamon Loingsigh
Light of the Diddicoy
Exile on Bridge Street

Aram Saroyan
Still Night in L.A.

Richard Vetere
The Writers Afterlife
Champagne and Cocaine

MEMOIR & BIOGRAPHY

Nassrine Azimi and
Michel Wasserman
Last Boat to Yokohama:
The Life and Legacy of
Beate Sirota Gordon

James Carr
BAD: The Autobiography of
James Carr

Richard Katrovas
Raising Girls in Bohemia:
Meditations of an American Father;
A Memoir in Essays

Judith Malina
Full Moon Stages: Personal
Notes from 50 Years of The Living
Theatre

Stephen Spotte
My Watery Self:
Memoirs of a Marine Scientist

HUMOR

Peter Carlaftes
A Year on Facebook

PHOTOGRAPHY-MEMOIR

Mike Watt
On & Off Bass

SHORT STORY ANTHOLOGY

Dark City Lights: New York Stories
edited by Lawrence Block

Have a NYC I, II & III:
New York Short Stories;
edited by Peter Carlaftes
& Kat Georges

Crime Plus Music:
The Sounds of Noir: An Anthology
of Music-Based Noir
edited by Jim Fusilli

Songs of My Selfie:
An Anthology of Millennial Stories
edited by Constance Renfrow

This Way to the End Times:
Classic Tales of the Apocalypse
edited by Robert Silverberg

MIXED MEDIA

John S. Paul
Sign Language: A Painter's
Notebook (photography, poetry
and prose)

TRANSLATIONS

Thomas Bernhard
On Earth and in Hell
(poems of Thomas Bernhard
with English translations by
Peter Waugh)

Patrizia Gattaceca
Isula d'Anima / Soul Island
(poems by the author
in Corsican with English
translations)

César Vallejo | Gerard Malanga
Malanga Chasing Vallejo
(selected poems of César Vallejo
with English translations
and additional notes by
Gerard Malanga)

George Wallace
EOS: Abductor of Men
(selected poems of George
Wallace with Greek translations)

DADA

Maintenant: A Journal of
Contemporary Dada Writing & Art
(Annual, since 2008)

FILM & PLAYS

Israel Horovitz
My Old Lady: Complete Stage Play
and Screenplay with an Essay on
Adaptation

Peter Carlaftes
Triumph For Rent (3 Plays)
Teatrophy (3 More Plays)

POETRY COLLECTIONS

Hala Alyan
Atrium

Peter Carlaftes
DrunkYard Dog
I Fold with the Hand I Was Dealt

Thomas Fucaloro
It Starts from the Belly and Blooms
Inheriting Craziness is Like
a Soft Halo of Light

Kat Georges
Our Lady of the Hunger

Robert Gibbons
Close to the Tree

Israel Horovitz
Heaven and Other Poems

David Lawton
Sharp Blue Stream

Jane LeCroy
Signature Play

Philip Meersman
This is Belgian Chocolate

Jane Ormerod
Recreational Vehicles on Fire
Welcome to the Museum of Cattle

Lisa Panepinto
On This Borrowed Bike

George Wallace
Poppin' Johnny

Three Rooms Press | New York, NY | Current Catalog: www.threeroomspress.com
Three Rooms Press books are distributed by PGW/Perseus: www.pgw.com